I0726954

Pawsitively A Purrfect Match

A Catmas to Remember

A Catmas to Remember

PEPPER MCGRAW

PMG Publishing

Contents

PUBLISHING HISTORY:
Shifter Christmas Howlidays | Naughty Nights Press | December 2022

Cover Images and Inside Images from Dreamstime:
Christmas Background © Anna Velichkovsky
Gray Cat Wrapped in Christmas Lights © Zsuskaa
Woman's Legs in Christmas Stockings © Kakigori
Cat and Christmas Tree © Afanasia
Paw Prints and Heart © Zsuskaa
Pawprints © Fourleaflover
Cat Tangled in Christmas Lights © Sofiia Kravchenko
Stylized Christmas tree with cat © Megapixelina
Cat ornamental © Megapixelina

ISBN 978-1-951247-30-0

Edited by J.L. Troughton
PMG Publishing

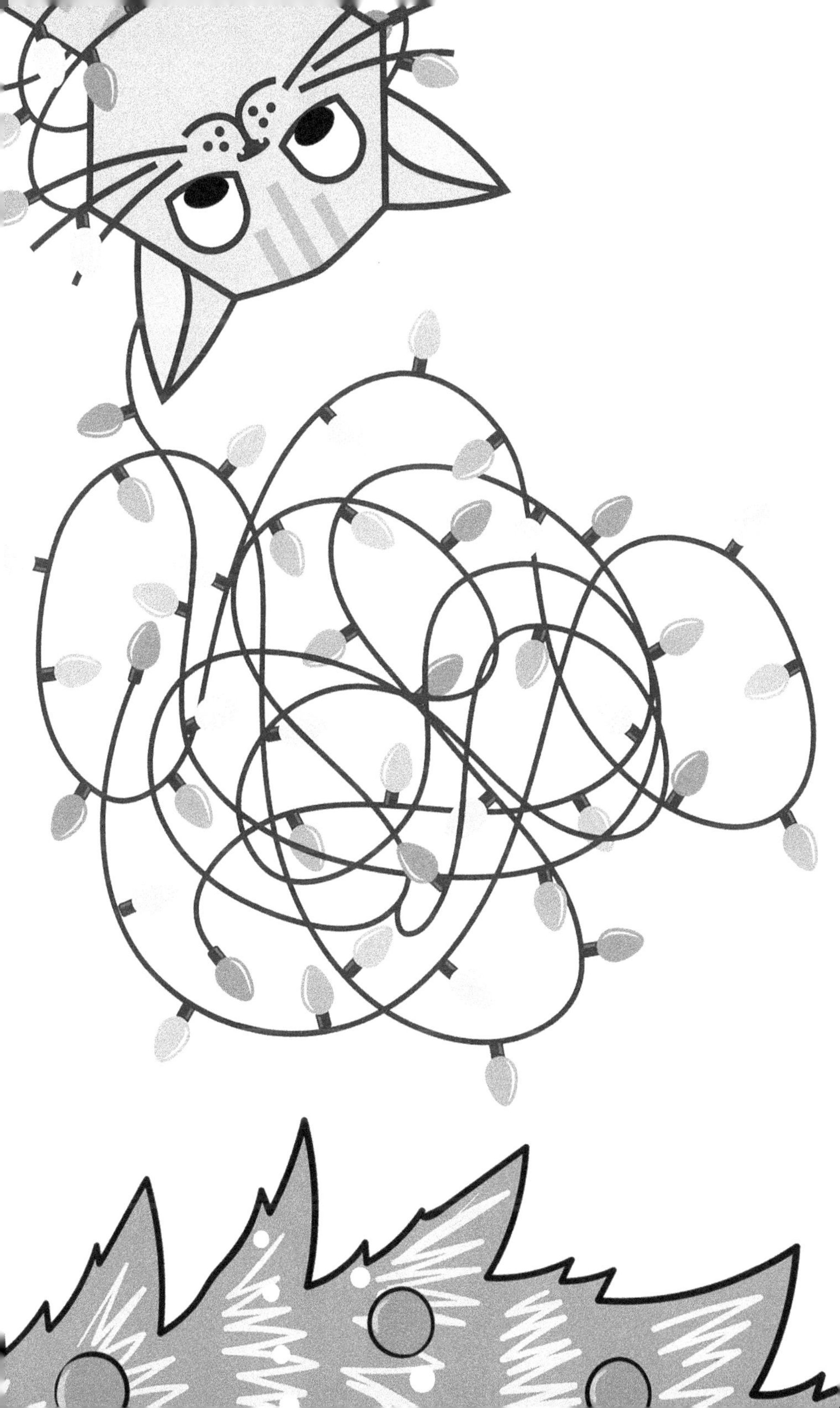

One

BYGUL WAS NOT happy about his latest assignment.

He might be the best matchmaker on the Pawsitively Purrfect team, specializing in matching humans with both their purrfect cat companion *and* their purrfect mate, but that didn't mean he could work miracles.

And this latest case would definitely require a miracle.

Most of the time, Bygul focused on homeless cats and kittens and didn't bother with those already scooped up by human rescue organizations.

After all, the humans did an excellent job of fostering and adopting out the cats they conscripted into their rescues, which allowed Bygul and the other cats of the goddesses to focus on matching cats who hadn't come to the attention of human rescuers.

Of course, there *was* the occasional exception, but that

usually involved circumstance rather than intention. Like when Bygul's trainees matched a bear with an arctic fox who ran a cat rescue center. Of course, it made sense at the time to match the bear with cats the fox was trying to find homes for, but again, this was due to the circumstances, which were unique.

Once those matches were complete, Bygul expected all of them to move on. There was no reason to continue working to place the cats in the rescue center. That task belonged to the humans.

The goddesses, however, seemed to have a different plan in mind.

"This particular cat is quite the troublemaker," Freyja informed him.

"He's been returned *seventeen* times," Bastet said.

"And by humans who adore cats, no less," Ceridwen agreed.

"Seventeen—how is that even possible?" Bygul demanded. He couldn't imagine that the director of the center, Isana Meier, had screwed up that many matches. After all, the woman was outrageously protective of her rescues.

"The cat's an asshole," Freyja said.

"Entirely," Ceridwen and Bastet agreed.

"But that's simply the nature of cats," Bygul protested.

Freyja raised an eyebrow. "Yes, but this cat takes it to unprecedented levels."

"He's smart," Bastet said.

"And devious," Ceridwen said.

"And he knows exactly how to make life miserable for his humans," Freyja said. "He's in a league of his own."

Now Bygul was intrigued.

Not that he would admit it, of course. "He can't possibly be that bad. Any true cat lover would put up with all manner of assholery from a cat."

"Not this one," the goddesses chorused.

Interesting.

Bygul did enjoy a challenge, but there were limits. "And how exactly am I supposed to get this cat away from the rescue?" Normally he just took the cats, but those were cats living on the streets, fending for themselves, with no humans to worry about them when they disappeared.

"You're just going to have to work with the humans to find the perfect placement for this cat," Freyja said.

"Have you *met* Isana Meier? Talk about uptight! *She's* the asshole in this scenario. She'll never let that cat be adopted by just anyone."

"Of course not," Ceridwen said.

"And why should she?" Bastet asked. "Every cat deserves the purrfect human."

"Exactly," Freyja said. "So your job is to find that human and somehow get them into the rescue to meet the cat."

"It's not enough that they meet the cat. Isana Meier has to approve their application and believe you, me, that's never an easy—"

"Bears!" Soraya exclaimed.

Bygul jumped a little. He'd completely forgotten the recent graduates he'd trained were in the room.

Great.

Now they'd want to assist in this match.

"Oooh, yes, bears," Tivali said.

"What are you two going on about?" Bygul glared at them.

"Who better to adopt an asshole cat than shifters who are assholes all the time?" Tivali asked.

"I vote for the polars," Soraya said.

"That's a crazy idea," Muezza said.

Bygul completely agreed.

"It's not crazy!" Soraya exclaimed. "It's purrfect!"

"Those polars are always fighting," Bygul said. "Besides, don't you remember how adamant Isana Meier was about bears *not* being an appropriate cat companion?"

"Yes, but that was before she mated one," Tivali said.

"Besides the polars are family," Soraya said. "She'd never deny family."

These cats were delusional.

Isana Meier would deny the goddesses themselves if she deemed them unworthy.

"Well, we'll leave the four of you to figure out the details," Freyja said. "Bygul, you're in charge. If you can't find a match for this cat, I fear for his future."

Great. Way to pile on the pressure. "What's the cat's name anyway?"

"Shredder," the goddesses chorused.

Wonderful.

"No," Mason said.

"He needs a home."

"That may be so, but his home's not going to be anywhere near *my* precious babies."

Isana rolled her eyes. "They're not even kittens anymore. They're fully grown and thus, are capable of defending themselves."

"Against Shredder the Destroyer?" Mason demanded.

"Stop calling him that!"

"Look, you know I love cats, but *that* is not a cat."

"Really, Mason?" Isana glared at her mate. Some days, she doubted her own sanity. She'd had one rule and one rule only her entire life: *no dating bears.*

And now look at her!

Mated to one.

For life.

A stubborn, clumsy, rampaging, irrational *bear.*

"If he's not a cat, then pray tell, what is he?" she demanded.

"Best guess? A demon from hell."

Isana groaned. "Can't we just discuss this? I've exhausted every cat lover I know in three counties. *Everyone's* heard about Shredder. No one's willing to take him in."

Mason just stared at her.

"What? What's that look supposed to mean?"

He didn't answer.

"What?"

He just kept staring.

She *hated* it when he did that. "Just say it already!"

"I've already said it a thousand times."

"Oh, no. Forget it. I already told you, no. We're not foisting Shredder off on the shifters."

"I don't see why not. You've adopted out to shifters before."

"Those were exceptions, not the rules. You know I prefer adopting out to humans, Mason."

"Which makes absolutely no sense whatsoever."

"It makes perfect sense."

"Not to anyone who isn't you."

Isana let out a tiny growl of frustration. "Fine. Who would you suggest then?"

Mason's eyes lit up. "Really?"

"Yes, really. What shifter is going to put up with Shredder's antics and not eat him when he riles them up? Because you know he will."

Mason grinned. "One whose terror of his sister is so great, not even Shredder could cause him to risk her wrath."

"Huh?"

"It's already working!" Soraya exclaimed.

"Please. Like you didn't plant the idea of the polars in his head," Bygul said.

"Well, of course we did," Tivali said. "Wasn't that the plan?"

"No!" Bygul snarled. "The plan was for me to find the right human—the *purrfect* human—and then send them to the rescue to meet the cat. The plan was *not* to send the cat to a psychotic polar and I cannot believe Isana Meier agreed to it."

"Desperation leads even the strongest among us to take drastic measures," Tivali said coolly.

"Look!" Soraya exclaimed. "They're about to meet for the first time!"

Bryce had worked a double at the restaurant the day before and was sound asleep when the pounding on his front door began.

He let out a roar of rage that rattled the windows and shook the floor, but didn't bother to get out of bed.

His roar was usually enough to send even the most determined packing.

Unless they were family.

Or insane.

Or both.

The pounding began again, which told him it was probably family.

Either that or the nutcase next door.

Either way, he was ignoring them both.

He pulled a pillow over his head and tried to ignore the relentless pounding.

It finally stopped.

He smirked a little as he sank back into sleep.

Bam! Bam! Bam! Bam bam bam!

Bryce jumped so hard, he almost fell out of bed, then leapt to his feet with a roar.

Family!

It had to be family.

The woman next door might be crazy enough to risk his wrath, but he doubted she had the strength to make the windows rattle the way they did with that last knock.

It was probably Isana.

Only his sister would have the audacity to continue knocking despite it becoming clear he had no intention of answering the door.

"Bryce, we know you're in there!"

Yep. That was his sister all right.

There was a reason he'd taken away her damn key.

Apparently, that wasn't enough though.

He should have moved.

Out of the country.

Bryce stamped across the room and flung open the window. "What the hell is wrong with you?" He couldn't see his sister because the roof of the porch obstructed his view, but he knew she was there.

The roof shook a little as Isana stamped down the stairs, turned and glared up at him. "Get your ass down here, Bryce Meier. Right now."

"I worked a double yesterday. Now go away." He pulled his head back inside the house, slammed the window and turned away, fully intending to climb back into bed and continue ignoring his sister.

Bam! Bam! Bam! Bam! Bam! Bam!

Hands on hips, Bryce glared at his bed.

Surely she'd give up.

Any minute now.

Bam! Bam! Bam! Bam! Bam! Bam!

Bam! Bam! Bam! Bam! Bam! Bam!

Bam! Bam! Bam! Bam! Bam! Bam!

Damn her.

A more bearish arctic fox he'd never known.

Grabbing a pair of sweats, he dragged them on, then stormed out of his bedroom, down the stairs to the front door.

He flung it open and glared at his sister and—great—her grizzly mate.

"It's about time." Isana shoved her way past him and as she moved by, he caught a strange scent of something foreign.

He whirled to follow and found himself shoved aside as Mason Worcester pushed by him with his arms full of bags.

Damn grizzly!

Scowling, Bryce turned to slam the door shut, but Mason shoulder checked him aside and stepped back out onto the front porch.

Bryce let out a low growl, went to slam the door shut *again*, only to have it flung back toward him by a massive grizzly paw in human form.

Bryce barely stopped the door from connecting with his face as Mason shoved by for the third time, this time carrying a strange box by the handle. "Now see here," Bryce snarled, turning to follow the grizzly down the hall. "What the hell is—"

He stumbled to a halt when he reached the door to his guest bedroom and finally realized what he'd been smelling. "Oh, hell, no!"

"THIS IS GOING TO BE AWESOME!" SORAYA crowed.

"Are you insane?" Bygul demanded.

"Why do you even bother asking that?" Muezza asked. "You know she is."

Unfortunately, he was right. Muezza was also the cat of a prophet (though he was currently making love matches for the goddess, Ceridwen), so he probably had greater insight than most.

"Why didn't you foresee this and warn me?" Bygul glared at the prophet's cat.

Muezza just stuck a leg in the air and started washing himself.

After a few moments of pointed silence, he finally lifted his head to say, "I thought it was pretty obvious the minute they mentioned the word bears."

Bygul growled low in his throat, uncertain whether he was more irritated with Muezza, the bear-loving idiot cats, or himself.

After all, Muezza was right. He should have known the minute Soraya mentioned bears that he'd already lost control of this particular match.

Except—hadn't Freyja said he was in charge?

He was pretty certain she had.

And yet, look at the result!

Not in charge of a darn thing.

"This match is doomed," he predicted.

"Don't be ridiculous," Tivali said. "Everything's going according to plan."

"Are you serious right now?" Bygul snarled. "How can *that* possibly be anything close to your plan?"

The four of them peeked back into the polar bear's home, just in time to see Shredder launch himself at the bear with a furious yowl.

Soraya winced. "Well. There are always growing pains. Right?"

"GET IT OFF ME!" BRYCE SHRIEKED, WAVING AN arm at the demon from hell currently hanging from his shoulders where its claws were fully embedded.

"Don't hurt him!" Isana shouted.

"Hurt *him*!" Bryce howled. "Are you crazy?"

A giant thud shook the floor and walls as Mason collapsed, roaring with laughter. His guffaws shook the windows.

Bryce clenched his fists and took a step toward Mason, fully intending to maul the grizzly into a pulp, but the cat on his back chose that moment to sink his teeth into Bryce's neck.

Bryce let out a roar of pain—those teeth hurt!—and whirled toward Isana. "Get him off me now," he said to his sister through clenched teeth, "before I forget that I love you."

And that he feared her wrath should he "accidentally" harm the demon on his back.

Long moments later, after Isana had crooned soothing words to the cat and coaxed him to let loose of Bryce's neck and shoulders, Bryce was finally free and the cat was cuddled in Isana's arms.

From there, the demon glared at Bryce with what he swore was true malevolence.

"What kind of cat is that?" Bryce glared back at him.

"He's really a sweetheart," Isana said. "He's just scared."

"Uh-huh." Bryce continued his stare down with the cat. No way was he going to blink first. "Why is he here?"

"He needs a home."

"And?"

"I decided you were the perfect candidate."

"For what?"

"For adopting a cat."

"Are you insane? Just because your mate is some kind of grizzly weirdo, who frolics in fields with cats and kittens, doesn't mean I'm going to follow in his footsteps." Bryce narrowed his eyes and intensified his stare.

The cat just stared back, not even a tiny hint of fear on its face.

"Hey," Mason exclaimed. "I resemble that. Except for the field. And the frolicking. And the weirdo part. Obviously, you haven't had the opportunity to spend time with cats until now and Isana feels it's time we fix that situation."

Damnit!

Bryce was so startled by that ridiculous claim that he blinked.

The cat smirked at him.

Argh.

Not cool.

Bryce turned and stared at the grizzly.

"This is all *your* fault," he growled at the grizzly.

He couldn't *believe* he'd blinked!

That damn cat would never let him live it down.

"I don't know what you're talking about." Mason grinned at him. "You should be thrilled we thought of you."

"I knew it! We, my ass. You grizzly bastard, you're the reason that demon's in my house right now."

"Eh, I'm just along for the ride," Mason said. "Isana's the one who—"

Bryce launched himself at Mason and the two of them flew through the air and landed on his coffee table in the living room.

The table collapsed beneath the weight of two full-grown bears and Bryce blamed that on the grizzly.

"Bastard," he roared.

"Take it outside," Isana shouted.

Two

J ENNIFER WOKE WITH a groan.

What the *hell* was all that noise?

The air was filled with shouts and roars and bizarrely, yowls that sounded very much like an enraged cat.

As far as she knew, there were no cats living on this block —domestic, shifter or otherwise.

Another roar ripped through the air.

Ugh.

It was that damn cranky bear again, she just knew it.

She'd done everything she could to win over her next door neighbor, especially after she got her first whiff of the man and her wolf perked right up, practically giddy at the thought that this fine specimen of a bear might be their mate.

She'd brought him cookies when he first moved in.

He'd grabbed the baked goods, then slammed his door in her face.

It had happened so fast, she assumed he probably hadn't caught her scent and that's why he didn't try to claim her right then and there.

She wasn't worried though. She was sure her cookies would win him over—everyone loved her cookies—and when he came by to thank her, he'd realized she was his mate and their happily ever after would finally begin.

Sadly, that didn't happen.

Instead, she'd been walking across their lawns, headed back to her house when he'd flung open his front door and roared that she was trying to poison him before pitching the entire plate, cookies and all, at her head.

Luckily, she had fast reflexes.

She hadn't even had a chance to yell at him before he'd slammed back into his house, door firmly closed behind him.

So he hadn't liked her cookies.

Fine.

She wasn't going to give up, though.

She'd tried a cake next.

Her cakes were so fantastic, she had friends willing to clean her entire house and do all her yard work in exchange for just one slice.

She'd spent hours on his cake and had carried it over ever so carefully, admiring the scent and beauty of her master-piece the entire way.

You'd have thought the bear would be extraordinarily grateful to be on the receiving end of such culinary genius.

Sadly, he was not.

Instead, not five minutes after she'd reentered her house, he'd sent the entire cake pan, cake included, sailing over their fence from his backyard to hers.

She'd spent hours scraping icing off the back patio.

At this point, any rational human *or* shifter would have given up.

They'd have washed their hands of the psychotic bear and gone on with their lives.

Jennifer Montoya, however, was made of much sterner stuff.

And so she'd baked him brownies.

Then cinnamon rolls.

And finally, the ultimate in her arsenal—bear claws.

She'd wasted so many ingredients—and genius—on that idiotic bear and what had he done every single time?

Accused her of attempted homicide before launching her masterpieces back onto her property.

What was *wrong* with that cranky bear?

After the bear claws, she'd given up.

Well, honestly, who could blame her?

The bear was clearly insane!

And now he was interrupting her beauty sleep with his roaring.

Jennifer considered herself to be quite reasonable,

cheerful even. She never let people get to her and always had a smile on her face.

She avoided confrontation and was always willing to give people the benefit of the doubt.

She'd come to the conclusion, though, that this tactic would not serve her well in her dealings with the bear.

She needed to find her spine.

She needed to channel her inner beast.

No.

Not *her* beast.

His.

She needed her inner wolf to adopt some bear traits.

Jennifer stormed out of her bedroom, down the stairs and through the front door.

She stamped across the lawn toward the bear's home and the sound of a vicious brawl.

She'd just reached the bottom of the stairs leading to his front door when said door flew off its hinges and hurtled toward her.

Good thing she had fast reflexes.

Jennifer darted to the side and watched as the door hit the ground, skidded several feet and came to a stop, two giant men rolling around on top of it, roaring and punching each other like little children.

Movement to her left caught her attention.

A woman came onto the porch, a giant orange cat cradled in her arms.

Jennifer raised an eyebrow at the woman, who just shrugged.

"My brother and my mate," the woman said as she came down the front stairs to stand at Jennifer's side. " They really couldn't be more bearish if they tried. I'm Isana, by the way."

"Jennifer." As Isana's hair matched the sheer white color of her neighbor's hair, she assumed the other bear he was currently attempting to maul was Isana's mate.

"Do you think they're going to stop anytime soon?"

"Probably not." Isana settled on the front steps.

"I get why Cranky Bear's fighting."

"Cranky Bear?" Isana let out a hoot of laughter.

Jennifer waved a hand in dismissal. "He's *always* in a bad mood, but why is your mate fighting? I thought bears were supposed to be calmer once they mated."

"Oh, they are."

"Really?" Jennifer watched wide-eyed as Isana's mate lifted Cranky Bear high into the air and hurtled him across the yard.

Cranky Bear landed on his feet, skidded back several yards, then launched himself forward again.

Isana's mate met him in the middle of the yard and they clashed with a roar.

Cranky Bear lifted Isana's mate off his feet and flung him toward the road.

"Hey, now!" Isana shouted. "No throwing Mason into traffic!"

Cranky Bear just let out a grunt and raced after Mason. The two collided in the middle of the street and the brawl continued from one side of the road to the other.

"This is ridiculous," Jennifer said. "I'm getting a hose."

THIS WAS THE MOST FUN BRYCE HAD HAD IN A long time.

Who knew the grizzly could be this much fun? He'd have to mention this to his brother and cousins.

They could have fun tossing the grizzly (and each other) every which way at family gatherings.

It would be fantastic!

When Mason launched Bryce through the air for the second time, he knew exactly what to expect and let out a roar of laughter.

It was almost like being on a roller coaster!

Without the seatbelt!

He landed on his feet, skidded back, then launched himself forward again.

So. Much. Fun!

His forward momentum was halted by a faceful of water.

What—

He shook his head, spraying water everywhere, then lifted his hand to block the spray.

Who was—

Oh, great.

It was the nutcase from next door.

He stamped toward her, ignoring the water that geysered all around him.

He bypassed Mason who was rolling on the ground, hooting with laughter, and walked right up to Ms. Nutty until he towered over her.

She didn't even flinch, just continued to change the angle of the hose she held so that the spray was constantly aimed at his face.

His hand blocked most of it, but he was still getting completely soaked.

"Woman!" he growled. "What is wrong with you?"

She dropped the hose and glared up at him. "What is wrong with me? What is wrong with you? Making so much noise on a Sunday morning, you woke the entire neighborhood! Hear that? That's the sound of every animal in the vicinity protesting their wake-up call!"

Mason wasn't sure if she was referring to the hyenas down the block who were yipping and playing in their front yard or to the wolves scattered throughout the neighborhood, who were all howling like it was the full moon.

He glared at his neighbor, then transferred his glare to his sister, who sat on his porch steps, calmly petting the demon cat in her arms. "The only one to blame for this fiasco is sitting right up there on my porch." He stamped his way past Nutty McNutters, bypassed his sister and stormed around the house to the shed in his backyard.

He flung open the door and perused the front doors inside.

His beautiful oak door was now splinters on the front yard, which was fine. He was ready for a change anyway.

Let's see.

Cherry.

Hickory.

Maple.

Spanish Cedar.

Mahogany!

He hadn't had a mahogany door in a while.

He hauled it free from the shed, lifted and balanced it on one shoulder, then stamped around to the front again.

Unbelievable.

They were all still there.

Hanging out in his front yard.

Like they'd been invited or something.

His sister scrambled off the porch steps as he stamped toward her, hauling the door with him.

It didn't take long to get the door situated.

He just muscled it into place, bent the frame back into position, flung the old hinges aside, attached the new ones with a couple slams of the fist and that was that.

He had a new front door.

Frame looked a little bowed, but whatever.

It was a bear door and that was to be expected.

He whirled and glared at the shifters *still* hanging out in his front yard. "Still here? Time to go. Now!" He jerked open his front door, then jumped back as something orange streaked past him into the house.

"See you later, Bryce!" Isana called.

"What?" He whirled and glared. "Get back here and take that demon cat with you. Isana!"

She just waved and climbed into her mate's car and two seconds later, they were gone.

Movement caught Bryce's attention.

His psycho neighbor was *still* just standing there.

He was gratified to see she was as soaked as he was, though he tried not to notice how her tee-shirt clung to her in all the right places.

Hmm.

He debated for all of a minute—wrath of Isana vs. wrath of Psycho Cat—and decided he was willing to risk it.

"Need a cat?"

"OH, BOY. THAT WOLF DOES *NOT* LIKE THE BEAR AT all," Tivali observed.

"And the bear can't stand the wolf," Soraya said.

"I don't know," Muezza said. "I think the bear maybe likes her a little more than he wants to admit."

"Don't be ridiculous," Tivali said. "He's shown no interest at all."

"Well, he liked her tee-shirt," Muezza said.

"What's that supposed to—Ohhh. Really?"

Jennifer stormed back into her house.

The nerve of that bear!

Her wolf had to be wrong.

There was no way Cranky Bear could possibly be her mate.

First he rejected all of her baked delights.

Then he disturbed the peace of the neighborhood on a Sunday morning.

Then he had the audacity to try and foist his cat off on her.

Unbelievable!

Though the cat *was* kind of cute.

She'd even pet it a little, right before she went to fetch the hose.

He'd purred and everything.

And okay, so maybe she was feeling a *little* guilty for leaving that poor, innocent cat in the clutches of a clearly insane polar bear.

But still.

She didn't want a cat.

At least she didn't think she did.

She'd never had one before, and had never really spent any time with one—with the exception of the shifter cats she knew, of course—so she couldn't really know whether she wanted one or not.

Still, it would be kind of weird for a wolf to adopt a cat.

Interesting that the cat hadn't hissed at her or anything.

You'd think it would have treated her like the predator she was.

Maybe the cat knew she was mostly vegetarian.

Yes, yes, she'd heard all the jokes.

A vegetarian wolf.

Whatever.

There were just so many other protein sources available nowadays. She didn't see the purpose in hunting down some innocent little animal, just because she had a craving for meat.

That wasn't the point anyway.

That bear was the point!

That mean, cranky, psychotic bear.

Who was probably mauling that poor innocent cat right now.

She didn't want to get involved.

She wasn't going to get involved.

There was no way she was getting involved.

Bryce was on a hunt to find the stupid cat when someone knocked on his door.

Seriously?

He wanted to hope it was Isana back, already regretting having left the cat in his care, but there was no way his sister would ever knock so politely.

With a growl of annoyance, he stamped toward the door and flung it open, already rehearsing the scathing lecture he planned to deliver about knocking on a bear's door.

Before he could utter a word, the whirlwind from next door shoved her way past him and into his house.

"Where is he?" she demanded.

"Who?"

"The cat. You haven't already killed him, have you?"

"What?" Bryce slammed the door shut. "Of course not! What kind of bear do you think I am?"

She raised an eyebrow at him. "Shall I list off the personality traits?" Without waiting for an answer, she began ticking them off her fingers. "Cranky. Rude. Stubborn. Psychotic. And did I mention cranky?"

"I am not cranky!"

"Whatever you say, Cranky Bear."

"No. Absolutely not."

"Excuse me?"

"You are *not* calling me Cranky Bear."

"Well, I don't see why not. It's a perfect description."

"I am not cranky!"

"Whatever. Where's the cat?"

"What cat?"

"*The* cat!"

"Who the hell knows? It's hiding somewhere, just waiting to attack the minute my back is turned, I'm sure."

"Don't be ridiculous."

"Look, Nutters, feel free to take this cat home and adopt him yourself. I'm sure you'll have much better luck than me."

"Excuse me? Did you just call me Nutters?"

He shrugged. "It's a name."

"Just like Cranky Bear's a name."

"Look, I'll call you by your name if you call me by mine. How's that?"

"That works. So . . . what's your name?"

"You don't even know my name?"

"Do you know mine?"

Bryce had to think about that for a moment. Surely, her name was rattling around somewhere in his brain, but the only ones that came to mind were Nutcase, Nutty and McNutterson.

Surely those weren't her names.

"Fine. What's your name?"

"Jennifer Montoya. You?"

"Bryce Meier."

"Fabulous. So, Bryce, where's the cat?"

Back here already, were they?

This was getting ridiculous.

But hey, *Jennifer* was now inside his house, asking about

the cat, so maybe his plan to con her into taking Shredder wasn't a complete bust.

"Not a clue,' he said cheerfully. "I'm sure he'll come out eventually, so you can go ahead and leave now."

"You're not even going to try and find him?"

"Nope."

"But how are you going to make friends with him if you don't look for him?"

"Not planning to make friends." He flung open the door with a grin. "Have a lovely rest of your day."

She just glared at him from across the room. "There's no way I'm leaving that poor, innocent cat here alone with you, you–you–you–"

"Yes?"

"Psychotic, cranky bear!"

"You've gotta get some new material, you know." Bryce closed the door. "So you're just going to hang around?"

"Until I find that cat, you bet!"

"Works for me." Bryce gave her a huge grin.

Three

BYGUL WAS STARTING to see the possibilities in this match.

If they could just get the wolf to fall in love with the cat and the bear to fall in love with the wolf, everything would work out perfectly.

"Things aren't exactly improving between the wolf and the bear," Soraya observed.

"Not even a little," Tivali agreed.

So there were a few hoops they'd have to jump through. "It's not like we haven't worked impossible matches before."

"Yes, but those humans were reasonable," Soraya protested.

Muezza let out a huff of amusement.

"Seriously?" Bygul demanded. "You thought Isana Meier was reasonable?"

"She was just trying to protect her rescues," Tivali said.

"It was perfectly understandable. The bear was the unreasonable one."

"He was just stubborn, not unreasonable," Soraya protested, "and that worked in our favor!"

"True," Muezza said. "He wouldn't give up, which is how we managed to place so many cats *and* match an unmatchable."

"Hey now," Bygul protested. "Mason Worcester was not an unmatchable. I've said it before and I'll say it again—everyone has their purrfect match somewhere, and frankly, the match between Mason and Isana, two of the most stubborn humans alive, should be proof enough of that."

"Okay, fine," Soraya said. "That may be true, but are you watching those two in there? The wolf *hates* the bear."

"And the bear's not exactly a fan of the wolf either," Tivali said.

"He's just using her," Muezza observed, "to get rid of Shredder, which really makes him as unworthy a match as there ever was."

"I really thought Bryce would be perfect for Shredder," Soraya said.

"Yep," Tivali said. "It's like I always say: one good asshole deserves another."

"You do *not* say that," Soraya said.

"Well, I should," Tivali said.

"Regardless, Shredder deserves better than him," Muezza said.

"As does the wolf," Tivali said.

"Right then," Muezza said. "First task: get the wolf to take the cat off the bear's hands. Second task: find the wolf her purrfect love match."

Bygul let out a rumble of disapproval, but said nothing.

What would be the point? He'd clearly lost control of the entire thing.

"You do realize it's already December, right?" Jennifer demanded as she checked under the couch in Bryce's living room.

"So?"

"So where are your Christmas lights? Your tree? Your presents?" She stood and stared around the room, perplexed as to where one not-so-small cat could possibly hide in a house that just wasn't that big.

After a few moments of silence, she glanced at Bryce, who stood across the room glaring at her.

"Oh. Sorry. Are you Jewish? I should have thought before asking. Still, though, if you're Jewish, you should at least have a Menorah. Why don't you have a Menorah?"

"I'm not Jewish," Bryce growled. "My family celebrates Christmas."

"Well, then where are your decorations, for heaven's sake? Don't tell me you're one of those crazy humans who waits until Christmas Eve to put everything up, then takes everything down the day after Christmas."

Bryce rolled his eyes. "Don't be ridiculous."

"Excuse me?"

"Why would anyone go to all that trouble for just two days?"

"Exactly!" Jennifer cried. "It makes no sense! I've been decorated since right before Thanksgiving."

"Yes," Bryce said dryly. "I know."

"Really?"

"It's not like I could miss the wolf decorating party happening in your front yard."

Jennifer grinned at the memory.

The best had been when her cousins set up a volleyball net and they all played the wolf version of it while rocking out to a stream of holiday songs.

She would have invited the bear, but that was right after he rejected her cinnamon rolls and she hadn't forgiven him yet.

Of course, that was probably a mistake. If she'd invited him, all those joyful, Christmas tunes would have surely put him in a better mood.

Which gave her a brilliant idea.

Jennifer pulled out her phone and after a few taps had her Christmas play list called up.

She glanced at Bryce. "Speakers?"

"What?"

"Never mind." A quick glance around showed her where

he docked his phone. Right beside his stereo system. Convenient. She skipped over, removed his phone, replaced it with hers and hit play.

Within seconds, her favorite Christmas songs were transforming Bryce Meier's space from boring to rocking. "Woohoo! You have a great speaker system!"

She skipped into the kitchen, calling, "Here kitty, kitty, kitty."

BRYCE GLARED AT WHERE JENNIFER'S PHONE WAS now docked and somehow communicating with *his* stereo system.

How had she even *done* that?

He was tempted to turn off the music, but he didn't want her to leave until after she'd agreed to take the cat with her.

With a long groan, he headed for the kitchen, trying to ignore the sounds of the most traditional Christmas songs ever filling the air around him.

When he reached the kitchen door, he stumbled to a stop. "What are you *doing*?"

His crazy neighbor had taken over the kitchen and was in the process of dragging ingredients from his cabinet. "I'm really impressed. I wouldn't expect a bachelor to have so many ingredients for baking in his cabinet. Like to bake, do you?"

"I manage the Ice Box," Bryce snapped. "Of course, I like to bake *and* cook."

"I don't see the correlation." Jennifer grabbed a giant bowl and started dumping ingredients into it.

"You know. The *Ice Box.*"

Jennifer sent him a blank look, then shrugged.

"It's a *Shenanigans* restaurant."

"Ohhh. Shenanigans. I love the brand. Isn't it a little pretentious to give your restaurant a second name? Why don't you just call it Shenanigans?"

"Because then people won't know what it is," Bryce growled. "It could be a bar or a hotel or a mall or some tacky tourist shop for all they know."

"And The Ice Box somehow fixes all that?"

"Uh, yeah. It's the restaurant run by arctic foxes and polar bears. Shenanigans could be run by any paranormal out there, but The Ice Box makes it clear these are arctic shifters running things."

"If you say so."

"I do say so, and just for that, hands off my ingredients." He snatched his mixing bowl away from her, grabbed the lid from a drawer and popped it on top. He'd deal with that disaster later.

"Hey!"

"No cooking in my kitchen. Especially not when every-thing you produce is sheer poison."

"I beg your pardon!"

"I don't trust you not to contaminate my kitchen with your terrible cooking skills."

"Well, I never!" Jennifer whirled and stormed out the back door.

"Damn," Bryce muttered. He'd let her get to him and now she'd left without the demon cat.

Jennifer slammed into her house.

"What a jerk," she growled as she flopped down on the couch. "I can't believe I let him get to me like that." She leaned forward, grabbed her remote and turned on the television.

She needed something to keep her mind off that poor cat and her guilt over abandoning him to the cranky bear.

An hour later, she was deep into *Homeward Bound,* grinning at Sassy the cat's antics as she ran circles around the humans, when there came a knock at the door.

Jennifer leaned back and peeked through the curtains behind her.

"Ugh. What does *he* want?"

She stalked to the door and flung it open. "What now?"

"I haven't found the cat yet." Bryce sent her a mournful look. "But so far, he's destroyed my favorite pair of shoes and has stolen all of my remotes."

"*All* of them? How many do you have?"

"Too many to count. And I can't find a single one."

"So what do you want me to do about it?"

"Well, I figure the cat's taken over my place by now, so it might be better if I just moved in with you." With a jaunty grin, he slid past her, sauntered to the couch, grabbed her remote and settled where she'd been just moments before.

"*Homeward Bound,* huh? I approve." He pressed play and the movie started up again.

Jennifer scowled, closed the door, stalked over to the couch and snatched the remote back. "You're in *my* spot." She glared down at him.

"No problem." Bryce grinned up at her, leaned forward, hooked her around the hips and hauled her onto the couch beside him. "Relax. We're getting to the best part." He slung an arm around her shoulders and pulled her close.

Jennifer froze and glared at the TV, trying not to notice how warm and comfortable she felt leaning up against him.

Despite her best efforts, the storyline caught her attention again and she slowly relaxed into Bryce, hooked once more by the antics of Sassy, Shadow and Chase.

Twenty minutes later, Bryce exclaimed, "Are you crying?"

"No." She swiped her hands across her cheeks.

"You are!" He sounded amazed.

"It's just so sweet." She couldn't stop smiling *or* crying as the animals and people on screen had their happy reunions.

"If you say so." He chuckled.

"All right, that's it." Jennifer shoved an elbow in his gut as she stood. "It's time for you to head back to your house and play nice with the cat." She tried not to wince at the thought of the poor cat, left to the care and mercy of this clearly *un*caring bear.

"Aw, come on, Jen. Don't be like that."

"It's Jennifer," she said through gritted teeth. "Now get out."

"Seriously? You're going to make me go back to the demon cat's territory? You know he's already claimed the entire house."

"You're being ridiculous." Jennifer thought the cat had much more to fear from the bear than the bear from it.

"You do realize who this cat is, right?"

"What are you talking about? It's a cat, for heaven's sake. An innocent, sweet cat."

Bryce let out a hoot of laughter. "That's what you think. Isana may have snookered you, but she can't fool me. I know who this cat is. I've *heard* the stories."

"Oh, please. It's not like the cat's a shifter. How bad can one innocent, domesticated cat be?"

"Hmmm."

She didn't like the look on his face. Calculating and devious.

"Fine then. Prove it to me."

"*What?*"

"Prove to me that the cat isn't a demon from hell and I'll do my best to make friends with it."

"Why in the world would I spend my time trying to prove *anything* to you?"

Bryce grinned. "Because otherwise, I can't guarantee the cat's happiness. Indeed, his fate at my house is probably a grim one."

Jennifer scowled. Manipulative bastard.

She *knew* he was manipulating her. *Knew* he probably wasn't as bad as he pretended. Was about ninety-nine percent certain his sister would never have trusted him with any cat if he weren't at least a tiny bit trustworthy.

And yet still.

She couldn't stop thinking about the poor cat.

Ignored and unloved.

Hiding in the bear's house.

Too terrified to venture out.

Wasting away from terror and hunger.

The damn bear probably wouldn't even feed it.

Argh.

"Fine." Jennifer glared at Bryce. "I'm not sure *how* I'm supposed to prove the cat's not a demon though. I mean, *obviously* it's not a demon. So what *exactly* do you want from me?"

Bryce grinned. "Well, first, I think we should move the cat over here. That'll give you plenty of time to gather evidence of its innocence."

"Forget it."

"Aw, come on, Jen."

"*Jennifer.* And no." She eyed Bryce, then added, "But I'll

come over and help you make friends with him." She should have done that to begin with. Who knew what the stupid bear would do if the cat startled him later? Everyone knew bears were extremely high-strung.

"Yes!" Bryce grinned, leapt to his feet and hurried to the door. "Let's go!"

Jennifer followed with a groan, absolutely certain she was going to regret this decision.

"You're a genius, Muezza," Soraya said.

"You really are," Tivali agreed. "Very subtle."

"Right," Bygul drawled. "Because it's not unusual at all for every channel to be playing a cat movie. Or for cat movies to already be pulled up on all the movie apps."

"It's not like she even noticed," Tivali said.

"Yeah, and if she had, she probably would have thought it was a cat holiday or something," Soraya said.

"What are you talking about?" Bygul demanded. "Humans don't have cat holidays."

Muezza snorted in amusement.

"Well, they should!" Soraya exclaimed.

"They definitely should," Tivali agreed.

"Right, let's find this cat," Jennifer said as she entered Bryce's house for the second time that day. "Do you have any cans of tuna?"

"Gross."

"A polar bear who doesn't like fish?"

"Give me a break. It's not the fish, it's the can. Disgusting. If you want tuna, I'll get it fresh."

"Hmm. The cat might like fresh tuna."

"What?" Bryce roared. "You want to waste perfectly delicious, fresh tuna on a cat? Forget it!"

"Hey. If you want to make friends with this cat, some sacrifices will have to be made."

"Maybe I need to rethink this friends idea."

Jennifer couldn't help it. She laughed. "Get over it, Bryce. Now let's go coax that cat out of hiding,"

An hour later, Jennifer had to admit defeat.

The cat was clearly a genius at hiding.

Which meant they were going to have to bring out the big guns.

"You know what we need to do, right?" Jennifer grinned.

"What?" Bryce glared at her, clearly reading the glee on her face.

"Decorate."

"For what?"

"For Christmas, you idiot!"

"But why?"

"Because everyone knows cats love Christmas!"

Bryce just stared at her. "You're crazy."

"No, it's true. The minute you start hanging tinsel or holiday lights, cats come running. Boxes of ornaments? Nothing but a haven of cat toys. And an actual Christmas tree? Nothing but pure joy for cats. They can climb the trunk, hide among the needles, bat at the ornaments and cause general mayhem."

Bryce groaned. "Everything about that sounds like a nightmare. A nightmare that's Christmas-themed."

"Oh, don't be such a baby. Besides, you need to get with the spirit of the holiday. You've leaving it way too late to decorate."

"Christmas is weeks away still!"

"It's never too early to decorate."

"Besides, I never decorate."

Jennifer gasped. "What? What kind of animal are you?"

"A polar bear, I thought that was obvious."

"Even worse! Polars live near the North Pole. If that isn't a reason to decorate, I don't know what is!"

"Well, *I* don't live near either Pole and I'm not a fan of Christmas."

Jennifer almost fell over, she was so shocked. "How can you not be a fan of Christmas? It's the jolliest time of the year!"

"Uh, no. It's the busiest, most annoying time of the year."

"You need help. Way more help than I can provide." Jennifer started for the door. "Don't worry. I'll be back soon enough."

Four

"YOU KNOW, SOMEONE'S going to have to convince the cat to come out of hiding," Soraya said.

"I don't think he's hiding," Bygul said.

Tivali groaned. "Well, don't look at me. The last time I tried to convince an earthbound cat to do something, he peed on the head of the boyfriend of the woman I'd matched him to."

Muezza snickered.

"I mean, I guess it wasn't a bad thing. It did get rid of the jerk, but things were a little tense there for a while."

"Not helpful," Soraya said. "The cat's still hiding."

"I don't think he's hiding," Bygul said again.

"Is he still hanging out on the kitchen cabinets?" Muezza asked.

"I think he moved and is now hiding on the fridge," Tivali said.

"He's not hiding," Bygul exclaimed.

"So who's going to convince him to come down from where he's hiding?" Soraya asked.

"Trust me," Bygul said. "That cat is *not* hiding!"

BRYCE WAS NOT A HAPPY CAMPER.

He'd failed again!

He'd had this whole plan where he'd get Jennifer back to his house, find the cat and convince her to take it with her when she left again.

Unfortunately, the demon cat was nowhere to be found.

Bryce was certain the damn thing was wreaking havoc wherever he was hiding.

Their second search of his house had discovered giant rips in his bedspread, shower curtain *and* favorite hoodie.

Bryce wasn't even sure how Shredder had managed to get to his hoodie. It had been hanging in his closet behind a closed door. Now though, the door stood wide open and his hoodie was on the floor in shreds.

As far as Bryce was concerned, this was just more evidence that Shredder was not only a demon cat, but also a master of the dark arts.

It was now even more imperative to convince Jennifer to take Shredder to her place. The alternative was unthinkable.

What if the cat decided to shred his face—or worse, his dick—while he was sleeping?

In fact, the way Jennifer had talked about the ornaments being cat toys had made Bryce shudder as he imagined his balls serving the same purpose.

The cat had to go!

Time to call the one to blame for this fiasco.

"Isana," he barked into the phone the moment she answered. "You need to come get this demon cat right now."

"Now why would I do that, brother mine?"

"Because he's destroying everything I own!"

"Oh, please, Shredder's a sweetheart!" Her voice trembled with laughter.

"Isana, I'm warning you—"

"Shredder is homeless and it's Christmas, Bryce. He's been rejected *seventeen times.* Of course, it's going to take time for him to trust you. Just give him a chance, *please*?"

Damnit.

Now she was manipulating him.

Not cool.

Bryce let out a rumbling growl. "Not fair, Isan—aaaah! Get off, get off, get off, you crazy demon cat."

Bryce whirled in a circle, waving his arms frantically, attempting to pry free the cat attached to his head—where in the world had the damn thing come from?

"Isana, you miserable fox, this demon cat just attacked

me!" He shouted at his phone, which was currently across the room where it had flown when the cat landed on his head.

"Argh!" Bryce let out a roar as the cat dug its claws deeper into his scalp.

"Help! Isana, help!"

The only answer from his phone was the sound of roars of laughter—that damn grizzly was listening to his pain—which almost, but not quite, drowned out the tinkling giggles of his traitor sister.

"What in the world is going on in here?" Jennifer arrived into the chaos like a breath of fresh air.

"Save me, Jennifer. Please," Bryce begged. "Save me!"

"You guys should really learn to listen to me," Bygul said.

"Whatever," Soraya said.

"I called it, though, didn't I?"

"Yes, yes, you were right," Tivali said. "The cat wasn't hiding."

Muezza let out a snort of laughter. "Did you see the look on the bear's face?"

"I had no idea a bear's voice could go that high," Tivali said.

"Shredder's a really good name for that cat," Muezza observed.

"Perfect really," Soraya agreed.

* * *

"Oh my goodness," Jennifer crooned as she hurried toward Bryce and the clearly traumatized cat who was clinging to his shoulder and head. "You poor, sweet kitty."

"Poor sweet kitty?" Bryce exclaimed as a burst of laughter came from his phone, which for some reason was clear across the room on the kitchen floor. "What about me? I'm being scalped here!"

"Oh, don't be such a baby." Jennifer reached up to the cat and crooned, "Come here, my sweet darling. You don't want to hang out with the grumpy, cranky bear when you could be with the cool wolves instead."

Bryce let out a rumbling growl of pain as the cat wiggled, shifted and dug its claws deep. That growl escalated to a screech when the cat launched itself into Jennifer's arms, yanking those claws free.

One hand clamped to his scalp, the other to his left shoulder, Bryce stamped to where his phone had fallen and scooped it off the floor.

"Isana! Isana! Stop laughing right now. And tell that grizzly mate of yours I'm going to rip him limb from limb if he tells *anyone* about this fiasco!" He stabbed the end button on his phone and glared at Jennifer.

She snickered. She just couldn't help it. The bear was *such* a baby.

"I cannot believe you're giving that demon cat sympathy! Did you see what he did to my shoulder?" Bryce pointed to the holes in the left shoulder of his tee-shirt. It would never be the same again!

Jennifer rolled her eyes. "Give me a break. Your bear skin is so thick, I bet he didn't even draw blood."

Bryce let out a gasp of outrage. "He most certainly did too! Look." He pulled his shirt away from the shoulder and turned it so she could see the underside of it. "Right there." He pointed to a tiny dot next to one of the holes. "Blood!"

"Yes," Jennifer drawled as she peered at the minuscule dot that really could be almost anything, though the faintest scent of iron meant the bear was *probably* right. Still, the teensy-tiny dot was barely noticeable. "I can see you're just *gushing* blood. We should probably wrap the wound, get you to the doctor for some stitches."

Bryce scowled. "That's not the point! Just because shifters heal fast doesn't mean it didn't hurt."

Jennifer grinned. "I'm sure it did hurt, but that's what you get for scaring him."

"I didn't scare him!"

"How do you know? Why else would he have jumped on your head like that?"

"Uh, because he's a demon cat. You *do* know who you're holding right now, right?

"Yes, an innocent, sweet, purring cat. He's adorable."

Jennifer gave him a scratch under his chin and grinned as the cat's purrs escalated in both sound and frequency.

"It's *Shredder*." Bryce shuddered. He couldn't believe his sister had brought that insane, psycho cat to her brother. Where was the loyalty?

Jennifer froze in the act of petting the purring cat. "Shredder?"

The cat, whose eyes had been closed in joy at the petting, opened those eyes and stared at her.

Holding her breath, Jennifer began to slowly pet him again.

When his eyes closed and his rumbling purr started up again, she released a long, slow exhale. "Not the Shredder I've heard stories about though. I mean, that cat's been placed in human communities, not with shifters, so it can't be the same cat. Right?"

The bear grinned at her.

She *really* didn't like the look on his face. Smug and superior and just a little bit wicked.

"You do realize my sister runs the Cat Rescue Center over in Pleasantville, right?"

Jennifer twitched, but quickly resumed petting the cat.

Pleasantville was a human town.

And she was pretty sure the Center he was referring to made the majority of its placements in human homes.

Why would a shifter work there?

"Isn't that the Center responsible for placing Shredder, not *this* Shredder—" *Please*, let it be any other cat but this

Shredder. "—in seventeen homes over the last three months? *Human* homes?"

Bryce grinned, clearly entertained at her dawning horror. "Yes. *That* Center. And yes. *That* Shredder."

"Oh, no. No, no, no, no, no. Why would your sister place him in the shifter community? It makes no sense."

"Because the humans clearly cannot handle this particular cat."

"And shifters *can*? I mean, okay, we do heal faster, but I think the chances of the cat surviving are probably lower among shifters than humans, at least if all the stories about him are true. I heard he shredded the entire lingerie collection of one of his owners."

Bryce nodded.

"She was a lingerie model. She'd collected those pieces for years. They were from the best designers in the industry."

"Yep."

"I heard he peed inside the violin of a concertmaster."

"Aimed it perfectly, so the stream poured into the holes. Apparently, the violinist didn't discover it in time. The pee soaked into the wood, warped it. Violin never sounded the same."

"Smell was probably worse," Jennifer muttered. She grimaced at the thought of that poor violinist lifting his prized instrument to rest under his chin, only to get a whiff of Shredder's gift.

"According to Isana, Shredder's incredibly smart. He waits until he knows exactly what his humans value the most and then he destroys it. No matter what it is. Until then, he just shreds all the ordinary things in the house, like my curtains and my hoodie, my pillows and my shoes."

"That's sounds really—"

"Psycho?"

"Sad. Doesn't Shredder want a home?" She looked down at the cat sprawled in her arms, purring up a storm. She couldn't even imagine this sweet cat doing all those terrible things.

"Isana thinks he doesn't trust the humans not to send him back, so he makes them do it before he gets too attached."

"Awww. Poor baby." She leaned over and placed a kiss on his forehead.

Shredder let out a rumbling purr.

"Seriously?" Bryce demanded. "You're bonding with the psycho cat right now?"

"He's not psycho. He's just misunderstood!"

A POUNDING SOUND CAME FROM THE FRONT OF THE house, followed by a male voice bellowing, "Yo, Jennifer!"

"Finally. They're here!" To Bryce's horror, Jennifer shoved the cat into his arms as she raced past.

"Wait!" Holding the cat as if it were a ticking bomb, Bryce carefully set it on the kitchen table and leapt away.

Shredder opened one eye, bared his fangs and hissed at Bryce, then closed his eyes and went back to sleep.

"Hurray!" Jennifer cried from the front room. "It's as cute as I hoped."

With no small amount of dread, Bryce left the cat behind and followed Jennifer's voice to the front door, only to stumble to a halt at the sight of two wolves muscling an enormous furry statue into the entryway of his home.

"What in the world is that—that monstrosity?" Bryce demanded.

"Isn't it obvious?" Jennifer asked.

"You're not leaving it there!" Bryce exclaimed.

"Of course we are," Jennifer said. "This is the perfect spot for him. Right here in your entryway. He'll be the first thing your guests see when they step into your home."

"That's what I'm afraid of," Bryce grumbled.

"But why? He's the perfect welcoming committee!"

"You *do* realize I'm a polar bear, right?" Bryce demanded.

"Yes. So?"

"So, *that's* a black bear!"

"And he's adorable, don't you think?"

"I definitely think so," one of the wolves said.

"Of course, you do," Bryce said. "You're a damn wolf, just like her. And who are you anyway?"

"Oh, right. I'm Nick, Jenni's cousin, and this is our friend, Wyatt."

"Hello. It's *Jennifer*."

Nick rolled his eyes at Bryce. "So where should we put the other stuff?"

"What other stuff?" How in the world had he lost control of his own home? When had he given permission to Jennifer to decorate his entryway? And how was *that* helping him with his cat situation? He just didn't get it.

"I told you. You need help," Jennifer said. "More help than I can provide alone, so I called in the recruits. We're getting your house decked out for the holidays."

"Yay!" Nick exclaimed as he headed out the front door, Wyatt on his heels. "Ryan! We're ready for—"

"Be right back!" Jennifer sang as she followed her cousin outside.

Bryce groaned.

He hadn't quite caught what Nick claimed they were ready for, but he was quite sure it was nothing he wanted inside his house.

He eyed the front door, then the black bear who stood across from it, sporting a Santa hat, a scarf and a sign that said "Beware of Bears!"

"I could just close the door," Bryce said to the bear. "Lock everyone out. Course then I'd be stuck with the cat."

The bear had no reply.

How ridiculous.

He'd been reduced to chatting with a giant, toy bear as if it were real.

He groaned and stepped out onto the front porch,

knowing even as he did so, he was going to regret the decision not to just lock everyone out.

When he caught sight of his yard, he stumbled to a stop, certain he had to be hallucinating.

His front yard was full of wolves—the same ones he'd seen at Jennifer's house a couple weeks before, stringing Christmas lights everywhere.

Unfortunately, they appeared to be continuing that nightmare job, but on his property this time instead of hers.

"Oy! What are you doing?" Bryce stormed down the porch stairs and headed for Jennifer, who appeared to be directing the chaos. "Are you seriously trying to make my house look like yours?" He waved an arm at Jennifer's front yard, where insanity had exploded Christmas all over the place.

There were Christmas lights everywhere—on the roof, on the porch railings and ceiling, on the tree in her front yard and the bushes against the house.

That wasn't the worst of it, though.

No.

She'd also decorated the tree in her front yard. Never mind that it wasn't a pine tree. That hadn't stopped her.

Nope.

The squirrels and birds had a heyday eating all the popcorn and nuts she'd strung all over the tree.

Every time Bryce thought the insanity of the wildlife channel was over—because everything had been eaten, of course—Jennifer decorated the tree again and the squirrels and birds were back.

Worse than that, though, was the ginormous sleigh complete with Santa and reindeer that filled the majority of her yard.

"Uh, yeah," Jennifer said, the word *duh* clearly implied in the tone of her voice. "I mean, look at my yard!"

All the wolves paused in their work to turn and stare at Jennifer's yard, then let out a massive cheer.

"Obviously, my yard is awesome," Jennifer said. "Don't worry, though. No need to be jealous. We wolves have you covered."

Bryce could see that as there were wolves all over his property, stringing lights and nuts and popcorn everywhere.

"How is this helping with the cat?" Bryce growled. "That's all I need your help with. Not Christmas decorations."

"Oh, the outside isn't for the cat." Jennifer led the way back into the house. "*That's* for the cat!" She pointed into his living room.

Bryce took one look and groaned. "Where did *that* come from?"

"Just hauled it in, dude," Nick said from where he, Wyatt and a third wolf were wrestling a giant Christmas tree into a stand.

Bryce stalked over and sniffed at the tree. "It's not even real!"

"Of course not," Jennifer said. "You have to wait until

right before Christmas to get the real thing—well assuming you're not going to be a heathen and chop it down. You want it still healthy when you transplant it back into the earth, which means you can't keep it up very long. Basically, if you want a tree for the entire season and don't want to kill one to make that happen, fake's the only way to go."

"But I don't want one for the entire season. I don't even want one at all!"

"Dude," Nick said. "You're a bummer. Who doesn't want a Christmas tree at Christmastime?"

"Only Cranky Bear," Jennifer said.

"No." Bryce glared at her. "We're not starting that up again."

Jennifer grinned. "Anyway, is it stable, Nick?"

Two of the wolves backed away from the tree while Nick grabbed hold of the trunk and shook it. He then stepped away and the tree—miracle of miracles—stayed upright.

"Awesome!" Jennifer cheered. "And here comes Shredder, just in time to check it out."

"Shredder?" the wolf Bryce hadn't yet met exclaimed. "Tell me that's not the Shredder Isana's been pawning off on every human she can find."

"Don't be ridiculous, Ryan," Nick said. "Isana wouldn't place him with—hold on a minute." He pointed a finger at Bryce. "You're a polar bear."

"Isana's his sister," Jennifer said.

"Oh, shit," Wyatt said.

All three wolves darted away from the Christmas tree,

Nick vaulting over the couch in the process, all in an attempt to get out of the path of the giant, orange tabby currently stalking across the living room floor, headed for the tree.

Shredder circled the tree's trunk twice, gave it a sniff once, then settled at its base, lifted a leg and began to bathe himself.

Bryce rolled his eyes. "Even the cat knows the tree is fake."

Five

"POOR SHREDDER," SORAYA said.

"Are you serious right now?" Bygul demanded. "Poor Bryce! I'm beginning to see why so many humans returned this cat."

"He just wanted Bryce to play with him," Soraya protested.

"By biting his toes?"

Muezza huffed in amusement.

"It's a time-honored cat tradition," Soraya said.

"That's not true," Bygul said, glancing at the other cats, who seemed to be avoiding his gaze. "Tivali?"

"Well..."

"There's no way that's a tradition, even among earthbound cats," Bygul said. "Feet are gross."

"Not when they're moving under the blankets," Soraya said.

"I have to agree," Tivali said. "Chasing toes in the middle of the night can be quite entertaining."

They had to be wrong. "No self-respecting cat would ever bite a human toe. Right, Muezza? Muezza?"

"Eh…" Muezza lifted a paw to scratch at his chin. "Maybe I've chased a toe or two in my time, but I don't actually eat them."

"Well, of course not!" Tivali exclaimed.

"Right," Soraya said. "The point is to catch them, not eat them."

"You three make me ashamed of the species," Bygul said.

"Are you seriously standing there telling us that you've never, not even once, chased after Freyja's feet?" Tivali demanded.

Bygul had a sudden memory of himself as a kitten bounding after Freyja, but that didn't really count, did it?

He'd just been following her.

He certainly hadn't been *aiming* for her toes when he just happened to land on them.

"You have!" Soraya crowed.

"If I did, it was a long time ago," Bygul said severely. "And nothing like the game Shredder was playing with Bryce's toes." Bygul shuddered at the memory.

"Yeah," Tivali said. "Shredder's in a league of his own."

JENNIFER WOKE FULL OF ENERGY THE NEXT morning. She'd been feeling a bit insulted the night before when she'd left Bryce's house.

After all, he hadn't seemed to appreciate all the effort she and her friends and family had gone to on his behalf.

Nick and Ryan had gone shopping for Christmas lights, Wyatt had picked up giant containers of nuts and the rest of them had brought over enough popcorn to feed the squirrel population of the neighborhood through the new year.

Nick had even convinced his boss, Kate, to loan them the black bear, not that Jennifer believed it was much of a sacrifice on Kate's part.

Jennifer only knew about the bear because Nick had told her stories for years about the black bear that was constantly being passed around the offices at The Worcester Group in Worcester Falls.

It had become a bit of an inside joke, where the bear would appear either outside a room where Mason Worcester, CEO of The Worcester Group, had recently gone on a rampage, something he apparently did quite often, or outside someone's office as a warning to others that the person inside might be the victim of a bear rampage at any moment.

Now that Nick's office was no longer located at the headquarters in Worcester Falls, but instead was inside an auto mechanic's shop—weird—those stories had dwindled over the past year until just last month when the black bear appeared inside the auto mechanic's shop at the base of the stairs leading to Kate's office.

Apparently, Kate was not amused, though her panther mate, Jefferson, and Nick and the other wolves, most definitely were.

Jennifer figured Kate had probably been thrilled to pass the bear on to someone else, even better if it was to a bear not at all associated with The Worcester Group.

In any case, Bryce Meier had been no more appreciative of the black bear than Kate had been, which in retrospect, Jennifer should have expected that reaction.

Still, he could have been polite about it.

And the lights were magnificent, yet somehow he didn't appreciate those either.

The night before, Jennifer had been a bit put out, but this morning, she was just more determined than ever.

So fine.

He didn't like the black bear.

Weird, but whatever.

She'd just have to find something better.

Something bigger.

Something way more impactful.

With this in mind, she made an emergency call to Nick and Ryan and made arrangements to meet them at the hardware store.

"He never should have given in to the yowling," Soraya said. "If Bryce had just kept his bedroom door closed, he wouldn't be limping this morning."

"I don't think it was the yowling that finally got him to open the door," Bygul said.

"I have to agree," Tivali said.

"It was definitely the crash," Muezza said.

"Crash*es*," Tivali said.

"True," Muezza agreed. "He ignored the first several."

"I'm a bit worried about Shredder's future," Soraya said. "The bear may just tear him limb from limb when he gets a look at his stereo system."

Bygul winced. "Let's just hope he doesn't notice."

"That would require a miracle," Tivali said.

"Well, we *are* the cats of goddesses," Bygul pointed out.

"I just don't think we're that good," Muezza said.

Looking at the level of destruction in the bear's living room, Bygul had to agree.

Bryce had finally gotten to sleep by putting on a pair of sweats and ski pants, two pairs of socks holding the bottom of the pants in place, a long-sleeved tee-shirt covered by a hoodie (with the hood up of course) a scarf wrapped entirely around his face (to protect his extremely vulnerable nose), ski mittens and on top of it all, a blanket he'd rolled himself into like a burrito.

Of course, he'd also had to kick the air conditioning down from its usual 60 degrees to just above freezing.

And still it was hot as Hades under all those layers.

The only thing that allowed him to finally fall asleep?

Sheer and utter exhaustion.

Also, the cat had apparently lost interest (finally) in his toes and had fallen asleep on top of his feet.

Unable to move for fear of waking the beast, Bryce had finally, just as the room was starting to brighten from the rising sun, fallen asleep.

He didn't know how long he'd been asleep when the pounding woke him.

He jerked upright and realized the cat was still lying across his feet, but was now wide awake, staring at him.

Bryce went to point a finger at the cat in warning, only to realize he was still wrapped up like a burrito and his arms weren't going anywhere.

Long moments passed as Bryce struggled to unroll himself from the blanket while simultaneously avoiding the cat whose pounces and swipes clearly signaled the end to the peace that had fallen around five o'clock that morning.

Staggering to his feet, Bryce stumbled toward the bedroom door, every step dogged by the determined cat, who kept swiping and lunging at Bryce's feet and legs.

Bryce lurched into the hallway, down the stairs and

toward the front door, where the pounding continued unabated.

What was wrong with people?

Bryce reached for the door, only to realize he was still wearing those stupid snow mittens.

He wrestled them off his hands, then jerked open the door. "What?"

"Good morning, Bryce!" Jennifer's voice was full of cheer, which just made Bryce even grumpier.

"There's nothing good about this morning," he growled. "The demon cat kept me awake all night long. I need coffee." He turned and stumbled toward the kitchen, ignoring the cat, who swiped at his ankles every few steps.

"It's freezing in here!" Jennifer exclaimed as she followed him into the kitchen. "No wonder you're all bundled up like you're living in the Arctic. Is your heater broken?"

Bryce stared at the coffee maker, willing it to produce the nectar of the gods just a little faster. "I've got the a/c on."

"It's winter! Why in the world—"

"Wow. It's so cold in here, I can see my breath." Nick walked into the kitchen, Wyatt at his side. "I think it's colder in here than it is outside."

"Your thermostat is set at thirty-five degrees!" Ryan called from the hallway.

"Don't touch that dial," Bryce roared. "I'm sweltering in here."

"Dude, far be it for me to tell a man how to dress," Ryan said as he appeared behind Nick, "but maybe if you took off a few layers, your electric bill wouldn't be so outrageous this month."

Wyatt grunted in agreement.

Bryce glared at the wolves standing in his kitchen, then looked down pointedly at the cat lying on the tile floor at his feet.

Shredder had his mouth clamped around Bryce's right ankle and his hind legs were scrabbling at Bryce's ski pants.

"Oh." Ryan snickered. "Maybe you should feed the cat, then he wouldn't be quite so peckish."

Bryce glared at him. "He's got food, but he's clearly more interested in chewing on my ankles."

"He's sooo cute," Jennifer crooned as she leaned over to scratch the cat's head.

Shredder had been growling in the back of the throat the entire time, adding a low menacing layer of sound to the kitchen, but the moment Jennifer touched him, he fell silent.

A moment later, the heavy sound of purring rumbled through the air.

"Aw, that's so cute," Nick said, taking a step closer.

The purrs instantly stopped and the growling resumed, this time at a louder decibel than before.

"Or not," Ryan said as he pulled Nick back to his side.

"Look, the cat clearly loves you," Bryce said to Jennifer. "Can you please just take him with you? He'll be much happier living with you, I'm sure."

"Forget it." Jennifer scooped Shredder into her arms and

grinned as he started purring again. "I'll come over every day and help you win him over though."

"Yeah, great," Bryce grumbled. "Thanks for nothing."

"Hey! Dude. Jenni's given you a lot, so how about a little gratitude?" Nick scowled at Bryce.

"A lot? You mean, like the black bear at the entrance of a polar bear's home? The fake tree that just looks stupid in the corner of my living room, that even the cat has rejected?"

"Yes!" Ryan and Nick chorused, both of them glaring at Bryce now.

Wyatt expressed his agreement with a fierce grunt and scowl.

"Plus you didn't even mention the front yard," Ryan said.

"Oh, I'm sorry. Are you referring to the lights I didn't ask for or the bird poop that will surely cover every surface as a side effect of all the nuts and popcorn?"

"Oh, you're an asshole," Nick snapped.

"Okay, hey, now, let's not get all bent out of shape," Jennifer said. "Bryce doesn't have to thank me for my generosity in sharing my awesome decorating skills with him. He can be as grouchy as he likes. After all, I would never ask someone to change their personality, not even Cranky Bear."

"No," Bryce said emphatically.

Jennifer grinned. "Besides, he hasn't seen the latest addition."

"Addition?" The dread Bryce felt in that moment was indescribable.

"Yes, it's so awesome! I know this is the decoration that will change your mind. Come on!" Jennifer darted forward, grabbed Bryce's hand and dragged him toward the door.

At this point, Bryce couldn't decide which fate was worse: trying to wrangle the cat without Jennifer's help in soothing the beast or dealing with Jennifer and her ridiculous decorating plans.

When he reached the door and saw what stood in his front yard, though, he *knew* which was worse.

"Is that an inflatable polar bear?" he demanded.

"Yes! Isn't it amazing?"

It was *not* amazing.

It was huge and tacky. "Why is it glowing?"

"It has built-in LED lights. Don't you just love it?"

Bryce had no idea what to say.

"He's speechless," Nick observed.

"Clearly overcome with gratitude," Ryan said dryly.

Bryce just shook his head, turned and walked back into the house, slamming the door behind him. His plan to go back to bed was thwarted almost immediately when he entered his bedroom and found Shredder had claimed the center spot.

With a low growl of annoyance, he stamped back out into the living room and stretched out on the couch, hoping when he woke, he would find this entire day had just been a bad dream.

"YOU WERE RIGHT," NICK SAID.

"About what?" Jennifer asked.

"Cranky Bear's the perfect name for Bryce."

"I know, right? I've been saying it all along. I've never met a crankier bear and that's saying something considering they're all a little bit cranky." Truthfully, Jennifer had never met a bear who *wasn't* cranky.

"It's saying a lot considering we've all met Mason Worcester," Ryan said.

Jennifer winced. She'd never witnessed Mason in a rage, but from what she'd heard, he could be pretty terrifying. "I suppose Bryce isn't *that* bad. Right?"

"Well," Nick drawled. "If we're using Mason Worcester as the guide for what constitutes a cranky bear—yeah, no. I wouldn't call Mason cranky. Insane, but not cranky. They're just not on the same level at all."

"He's right," Ryan said. "Mason's more an example of a homicidal, psychotic bear, whereas Bryce is just—"

"Cranky?" Jennifer suggested.

"Bitchy," Ryan and Nick chorused.

Wyatt let out a grunt of agreement.

Jennifer sighed. "I suppose I should go check on him, make sure he's okay." She hesitated. "Make sure the *cat's* okay."

"Right," Ryan said. "You know, I never thought I'd say

this, but I honestly think you should be more worried about Cranky Bear."

"No kidding," Nick said. "That Shredder's mean."

"And did you see the bear's get-up?" Ryan asked.

Nick snickered. "I can't believe all the layers he was wearing, just to protect himself from Shredder's claws."

"And teeth," Jennifer said.

Ryan and Nick laughed.

"Lunch," Wyatt grunted.

Jennifer laughed. "Okay, why don't you guys go grab us some food? Maybe from the Ice Box. That might help us win some points with Cranky Bear."

"Not a bad idea." Ryan slung an arm around Nick's shoulders. "Come on, Wyatt." He led the way toward their car, calling over his shoulder, "Good luck wrangling the bear."

"You're gonna need it!" Nick sang.

Jennifer rolled her eyes, dragged in a breath for courage and headed up the stairs to Bryce's front door.

Six

T HE FIRST INKLING Bryce had that he was no
longer alone was when the cat landed on his chest
and began kneading it with his claws.

"Yeow!" Bryce yelled.

He'd forgotten the blanket, the absolutely critical third
layer of protection from cat claws.

He reached behind him and grabbed one of the pillows.
Though it was tempting to use it as a barrier between the cat
and where its claws were currently embedded, Bryce knew
what was most important to protect and with this in mind,
placed the pillow strategically over his dick.

Long, endless moments of agony later, the cat was finally
finished walking in a circle while kneading Bryce's torso into
shreds, and collapsed on his side where he curled into a
ball and—

Bryce froze and stared at the cat.

What was he doing?

Surely he wasn't—

A loud purring sound rumbled through the air.

He was.

The cat was sleeping and purring!

This couldn't be right.

The cat was probably just messing with him, lulling him into a fake sense of security, right before he pounced.

Well, Bryce wasn't falling for it.

When the cat started up its aggressive behaviors, Bryce would be ready for it.

Any minute now.

Any minute.

JENNIFER COULDN'T BELIEVE HER EYES.

The cat was sound asleep on the bear's chest and the bear appeared to be asleep as well.

Not only that, but Shredder was *purring*.

Unbelievable.

Even as she was thinking that maybe she should just step out and leave the bear to bond with the cat on his own, Bryce's eyes opened and he scowled at her.

And there he was.

Cranky Bear.

"What's wrong, CB?"

A perplexed look crossed Bryce's face. "CB?"

She grinned. "Shorthand for Cranky Bear."

He scowled. "No."

She giggled. "I can't believe you're still in a bad mood. How can you be cranky when you've got a purring cat on your chest?"

"Quite easily, especially when that cat is Shredder. You mind getting him off me?"

Jennifer grinned. "What, are you afraid to do it yourself?"

"Uh, yeah."

Jennifer laughed. "Fine. Come here, baby." She picked Shredder up and cuddled him a moment before setting him down on the floor.

Bryce sat up and glared at her. "I can't believe you."

"Oh, for heaven's sake. What's your problem now? I just helped you, didn't I?"

Bryce surged to his feet, reached over the back of the couch and yanked the curtains wide. "*That's* my problem."

She looked out the window, then back at Bryce. "I don't get it."

"Why is there an inflatable polar bear on my front lawn?"

"Are you kidding me? Because it's awesome!"

"It is *not* awesome. It's ridiculous!"

"You're ridiculous. That polar bear is perfect!"

"You're insane. That's the only possible explanation." Bryce crossed his arms and glared at her. "You're insane."

"He's the *perfect* Christmas accessory for a polar bear's home!" Jennifer waved her arms and began to pace back and forth. "How can you not see that?" She couldn't believe how stubborn Bryce was. She stormed to the front door and flung it open. "Look at him! He's so big and white and glowing and he's got a Santa hat and a scarf and he's wearing ice skates! How can you not love him?"

Bryce stamped to the front door and peered out it. "He's wearing ice skates?"

"You didn't notice?"

"Hell, no, I didn't notice!" He flung open the door, stormed down the porch steps and stamped through the snow toward the polar bear. He glared down at its feet and let out a low growl.

She was right.

It *was* wearing ice skates.

Jennifer reached his side and Bryce's frustration boiled over.

He whirled and yelled in her face, "*Why* is the polar bear wearing ice skates?"

Jennifer took a step back, belatedly registering how annoyed Bryce really was. "Well, maybe he's a shifter bear."

"A shifter bear who ice skates in his shifter form?"

Jennifer shrugged. "Maybe."

Bryce's eyes narrowed and he stormed toward her.

She scrambled back, but he jut kept coming and suddenly he was right there, in her space, grabbing her shoulders, hauling her up on her toes and then—

He kissed her.

"WHAT IS GOING ON RIGHT NOW?" SORAYA exclaimed. "This isn't what's supposed to be happening. Why is he kissing her?"

Muezza snorted. "Isn't it obvious?"

"No!"

"I think it means he likes her," Tivali said.

"That's not possible. He's been so mean and grumpy and rude!"

"Probably because he likes her," Muezza said.

"I do not like this development." Soraya scowled.

Bygul just grinned. He'd seen this scene coming a mile away. It had just been a matter of time. At least as far as he was concerned.

Soraya, on the other hand, clearly did not agree. "I was rooting for Wyatt."

Bygul shook his head, certain he must have heard wrong. "Did you say *Wyatt*?"

"He's the purrfect match for Jennifer," Soraya said.

"How do you figure?" Tivali asked. "He never speaks. All he does is grunt."

"Yes, but he did pet Shredder on the head once and the cat didn't seem to mind."

"He did?" Muezza asked.

"Yep."

"When?" Bygul asked suspiciously.

"When Jennifer was holding Shredder."

"Were Shredder's eyes open at the time? Was he awake?" Bygul asked.

"No. Maybe."

Muezza made a scoffing sound in the back of his throat. It kind of sounded like he was about to cough up a furball.

Bygul took a step back, just in case.

"You do realize he probably thought it was Jennifer petting him," Tivali said.

Soraya looked disappointed. "I suppose. I still like Wyatt more than Bryce though."

"I thought you wanted a bear for Shredder," Bygul said. "This was your idea from the very beginning."

"That was before I realized the bears were so mean."

"How could you not know that?" Tivali demanded.

"You were right there with us when we matched both Kate Worcester and her brother, Mason," Bygul exclaimed. "How could you not have noticed how mean they both were?"

"Especially Kate," Muezza muttered.

"I suppose, but Mason loves cats. I thought Bryce would be the same."

"But Shredder isn't just any cat," Bygul said.

"I know," Soraya said morosely.

"I think we should go along with this development,"

Tivali said. "The bear and the wolf could be a wonderful mating."

"Or a disastrous one," Muezza muttered.

FOR A MOMENT, JENNIFER HAD NO IDEA WHAT to do.

The bear was kissing her.

She'd finally resigned herself to accepting that he would never, ever make a move, and now he was kissing her.

She was frozen in shock for a moment, but then it happened.

Heat snaked through every part of her being and she went from rigid in his arms to trying to climb him like a tree.

His tongue wrapped around hers and a flash of heat surged south.

She gave a little hop and Bryce caught her by the back of her thighs, spread them wide and wrapped her legs around his hips.

Jennifer squirmed closer, rubbing her aching center along his growing hardness and whimpered into his mouth.

Bryce started walking and the movement added friction that flashed more heat through her with every step.

He slammed her against something hard and moved against her in a way that simulated sex.

Jennifer flung her head to the side and mewled as he

continued rubbing against her, driving her closer and closer to the edge.

"Bryce!" Her eyes flew open as she broke apart into a million pieces.

When her senses returned, all she could hear was the heavy breathing of the bear who had her pinned to the side of his house.

"Oh, goddess," she whispered. "What the hell was that?"

She could feel him right up against her, hard as a brick, ready to go again. Or still.

Based on how rigid his stance was, still.

She slowly turned her head and looked up.

His eyes were on her, glowing with a wildness that made her heart pump faster.

"Bryce," she whispered, then reached up and laid a kiss on his clenched jaw. "Do you want to—"

The sound of car doors slamming interrupted what she'd been about to say and then she heard Nick's voice calling her name.

"Bryce," she whispered again.

He carefully stepped back and let her legs go.

She dropped them to the ground and he steadied her until she could stand on her own.

"Go ahead." His voice sounded like he'd been chomping gravel. "I'll join you in a moment."

She drew in a deep breath, the scent of their desire all around them, then nodded. She glanced down and her eyes widened.

Dear heavens.

She'd felt him against her so shouldn't be surprised at the bulge that threatened to burst through his pants, but she really, really was.

Impressed too.

"Go on," he said again.

She nodded. "I'll get rid of them if you—"

"No." Bryce shook his head. "It's all right. I'll be there soon."

THE WOLVES HAD SET OUT LAWN CHAIRS IN THE snow and were unpacking bags from The Ice Box when Bryce arrived.

"We're eating out here?" Bryce was surprised since it was rare to find other shifters who loved the snow the way Bryce did.

"Dude, it's colder inside your house," Nick said.

"I suppose it is," Bryce said. "Hey. Who let the cat out?"

"Oops," Jennifer said. "I might have forgotten to close the door behind us."

"No problem," Bryce said. "Maybe I'll get lucky and the cat will run away."

"Doubtful," Jennifer said. "Besides, Isana would never forgive you if you lost the cat."

Bryce let out a huff of despair and resigned himself to keeping an eye on the cat while it explored the yard.

Of course, Shredder, being the instigator he was, started trouble almost immediately by getting into a shouting match with a squirrel.

The squirrel chittered at Shredder and Shredder yowled and hissed back and the sounds just escalated from there.

The squirrel ran from one branch to the next of the tree and taunted Shredder until the cat lost his patience and made a lunging leap for the lowest branch in the tree.

The next thing they knew, the cat was chasing the squirrel all over the damn tree.

Jennifer got more and more agitated the higher the squirrel led Shredder.

"Shredder, baby, come on down now," she called up the tree.

"Eh, he'll come down when he's ready," Bryce told her, but apparently that wasn't good enough.

"You need to go up there and rescue him, Bryce."

"Hell, no. I am not a tree-climbing bear. I'm a polar bear and polars do not climb trees."

"But humans do. Please, Bryce."

"No way. There is no way I'm going up in that tree."

Five minutes later, Bryce was climbing the damn tree. He had no idea how he'd lived to full adulthood without ever climbing a tree and yet here he was, definitely old enough to know better, clinging to the trunk of a tree, trying to rescue a cat too stupid to know that it belonged on the ground, not hopping around in trees.

"Shredder," he snarled as soon as he judged he was close enough for the cat to hear him. "Get your ass down here right now."

Of course, the cat didn't listen. He just climbed higher.

Say what you will about polar bears, Bryce wasn't stupid. "I am not following you. That limb will collapse beneath me and we'll both end up falling to the ground. Only difference is you might land on your feet. Course you'll probably break all four of them from this height, but hey, keep climbing."

Bryce inched his way around and settled in a nook created by two giant limbs. "I'll just wait for you here."

"Did you get him yet?" Jennifer called up to him.

"Working on it," he called back. "Working hard," he muttered as he dragged out his phone and began playing a game of Solitaire.

Let the cat come to him.

Or not.

Maybe the cat would move in with the squirrel permanently and he'd no longer have to worry about losing his toes, nose or balls in the middle of the night.

A few moments later, the squirrel darted past on a limb just above Bryce's head and Shredder crept down to the same limb, where he crouched and stared at the squirrel.

Bryce quickly shoved his phone back in his pocket and stared at Shredder.

Shredder stared at the squirrel.

And the squirrel mocked them both, chittering and jumping up and down.

Shredder leapt down onto Bryce's lap and from there launched himself toward the squirrel.

Bryce managed to get his arms wrapped around Shredder at the very last moment and had just settled the cat against his chest when one of the limbs beneath him broke.

JENNIFER WAS PACING AROUND THE TRUNK OF THE tree when the sound of a limb breaking made all four wolves look up.

A bear roar rent the air as leaves, tree limbs and Bryce came thundering down.

Seconds before Bryce landed flat on his back in the snow, Shredder leapt free of his chest and landed daintily on his feet.

Snow geysered everywhere and Shredder leapt up, batting at flakes as they danced in mid-air.

"Are you okay?" Jennifer asked.

Bryce opened one eye, then the other. "So now you're worried about me? I notice you weren't worried when I climbed high in the tree to try and save an animal who always lands on its feet."

"Uh, guys," Nick said from behind them.

"Oh, please. Are you all right or not?"

Bryce sat up with a groan. "I'm sure I'm fine. As soon as my broken spine heals itself."

"Guys."

"Oh, stop it, you big baby."

"Jennifer!"

"What?" Jennifer whirled to glare at Nick.

"Your cat's stalking the bear."

Jennifer glanced back at Bryce, who had managed to climb to his feet, with a lot of groaning and sound effects, of course.

What a drama queen.

She looked around, but didn't see Shredder anywhere.

"Not that bear," Nick said. "*That* one." He pointed across the yard and Jennifer turned in time to see Shredder launch himself into the air and land on the inflatable bear's back.

For a moment, Jennifer feared the polar bear would collapse under the wrath of Shredder, but it barely moved at all.

Shredder reared back and pounced on the neck of the bear.

Again, the bear barely moved.

At that point, Shredder went nuts, racing up and down the length of the bear, from head to tail and back again, pausing every couple minutes to swipe at the bear with his claws and to attempt to take a bite out of its ass or to chew on its ear.

"Man, that bear can take a beating," Ryan said.

"Better it than me," Bryce grumbled.

At that moment, a loud whining sound filled the air as the polar bear began to collapse.

"Oh, great," Jennifer exclaimed.

"I've changed my mind," Bryce announced. "The cat can stay."

"You would say that," Jennifer huffed, then went to join Wyatt, who was already working to deflate the bear, so they could patch whatever holes Shredder had made and then re-inflate it.

"No really," Bryce called after her. "The cat can stay, but the polar has got to go!"

"Soraya!" Tivali admonished.

"What?" Soraya asked.

"There is no way Shredder's puny claws caused any damage to that bear."

"So?"

"So what's the deal?"

"I told you. I like Wyatt for Jennifer. Collapsing the bear was brilliant. Look! They're working together to fix it."

"Yes and while they're working together, Bryce is bonding with Shredder," Muezza observed.

"What?" Soraya exclaimed. She scowled down at Shredder, who for some reason had exchanged the collapsing bear for the real one. "But I'm not trying to match the bear and the cat!"

"Well, I am," Bygul said, "so good job."

"Harumph." Soraya plopped onto her side in frustration.

Why couldn't anyone understand what she was trying to accomplish here?

Jennifer—not Bryce—was clearly the purrfect cat companion for Shredder and Wyatt—again, not Bryce—was clearly the purrfect mate for Jennifer.

Seven

IT WAS THE kiss that did it.

Until that very moment, Jennifer had had her doubts. Sure, her wolf had been fascinated with Bryce from the very beginning, but Bryce clearly didn't return that sentiment, so she'd decided her wolf had to be off her rocker.

But then, *that kiss.*

That was when she realized it wasn't her wolf who was confused. It was *his* bear.

His stubborn, obnoxious, ignorant bear!

Apparently—at least according to Kate Worcester, whom Jennifer had called the night before, in desperate need of advice—bears didn't always know their mates right away.

In fact, bears were notorious for not recognizing them at all, which made any mating with a bear downright difficult, unless you were also a bear, in which case, the mating went from merely difficult to almost impossible, seeing as two bears had very little chance of ever figuring things out on their own.

It was why, Kate said, so many bear shifters were mated with non-bears. It was the only way to ensure the continuation of their kind.

While this explained why their mating failed to take off right away, it didn't explain why it continued to sputter *after* their kiss.

It was really quite infuriating.

After all, Bryce had been the one who kissed her—kissed her straight into an orgasm, in point of fact.

It seemed pretty logical, therefore, that after everyone left the night before, she and Bryce would continue where they'd left things off.

So she'd been completely unprepared for him to bid her goodnight before stalking into his house, Shredder in his arms, and slamming the door behind him.

She'd followed, of course, demanding, "What in the hell is your problem, Cranky Bear?"

He'd seemed surprised at the question at first, but then hadn't held back when informing her that she was, "A reckless, interfering witch, who had almost gotten him killed saving a cat who didn't need saving."

"I beg your pardon?" She'd been terribly offended, of course.

He'd gone on to inform her that he'd decided he no longer needed her help in winning over the cat—he'd managed that on his own, thank you very much—and that she should go back to decorating her own home with her ridiculous Christmas decorations and leave his alone.

At that point, Jennifer had lost it and called him, "A stubborn, idiot bear who wouldn't recognize a good idea if it bit you on the ass."

She'd then gone on to say, "And by the way, you're too stupid to realize it, but there's no way you won over that cat without my help. You wouldn't have been in that tree if it weren't for me and don't think I didn't notice how you cradled the cat to your chest as you fell. You can be damn sure Shredder's smart enough to have figured that out as well. So go ahead, act like a big jerk. You're not fooling anyone, least of all me. I'm not going to let you drive me away, no matter how big an ass you become."

He'd scowled and yelled, "Well, for the goddess' sake, why not?"

"Because, you idiot bear, you belong to me!" She'd screamed in his face, then had turned and stormed out.

Stupid bear.

He thought he could discourage her after that kiss?

Well, he was in for a helluva surprise.

She was just getting started on her mission to win over her mate.

"Yay! Wyatt's back," Soraya exclaimed.

"I wouldn't get my hopes up on that front," Tivali said.

"Well, why not?" Soraya demanded.

"Because," Muezza said, "Wyatt was the only one available to help Jennifer with the next phase of Operation Bryce."

"What does that even mean?" Soraya asked.

"It means she's decided Bryce Meier is her mate and she's going all out to convince him." Bygul grinned.

"That doesn't even make sense," Soraya said. "She calls him Cranky Bear!"

"Yeah, well, at this point, I think it's a term of endearment," Bygul said.

"That's just wrong," Soraya said.

BRYCE WAS ON THE MORNING AND AFTERNOON shifts at the restaurant the next day.

Normally, he thoroughly enjoyed it when he had the opportunity for two days off in a row since it happened so rarely. This time, though, he'd been delighted to get back to work.

It meant his home was safe from Jennifer's crazy decorating scheme, at least for one day, and for this, he was eternally grateful.

He wasn't as happy when he arrived at work and discovered in the two days he'd been gone, a mother cat had somehow sneaked into the restaurant with her five kittens and had claimed the area beneath the desk in the management office.

His office.

His desk.

"What the hell?" he bellowed. "You just let them stay?"

"Isana told us the mama cat chose a place she felt was safe for her kittens and we shouldn't move them yet," his brother Zach explained.

"Not cool," Bryce said. "What are we supposed to do with them?"

Zach shrugged. "Feed them, I guess."

"Great." Bryce scowled his way through the rest of his shift, thoroughly annoyed that he was now somehow caring for cats both at home *and* at work.

He knew exactly how this was going to go.

It was entirely too predictable.

Somehow Isana would manipulate one of them into taking the cats into their own home. Well, it wasn't going to be him. He'd already been manipulated once.

She could just choose someone else next time.

He spent the rest of his shift plotting how to pawn the cats off on someone else in the family, preferably Zach or one of their many cousins.

Between the cats and discovering spices missing from their latest delivery, Bryce was in a terrible mood by the time he left the restaurant and headed home that evening.

To say he wasn't in the right frame of mind to discover

the Christmas scene on his front lawn had expanded while he was away was an understatement of epic proportions.

JENNIFER HAD JUST SETTLED ON THE SOFA WITH A good book when the pounding on her door began.

She jumped, then leaned over the back of the couch to check through the front window.

The wolf inside her gave a yip of excitement at the sight of Bryce on her front porch.

Jennifer was a little too practical, though, to feel any sort of optimism, and instead, walked to the front door with a healthy dose of trepidation.

She couldn't imagine why her mate wouldn't like the latest addition to his decorations, but then she still didn't understand what his objections were to the polar bear, the lights or the black bear.

So basically, she had absolutely no faith that he would respond to her gift with anything but horror.

Still, hope sprang eternal.

She flung open the door and beamed at her mate. "Bryce! I've missed you." She flung herself forward and managed to grab hold of his waist in a strong hug before he could stop her.

Of course, the hug only lasted a second before Bryce had her set away from him and was frowning down at her sternly. "You do know that polar bears live in the Arctic, right?"

"Of course I do," she beamed up at him. "Well, real polar bears anyway. Shifters live wherever."

"Are you suggesting there are penguin shifters?"

Jennifer's eyes widened. "I don't know. I suppose there could be." She thought about it a moment. "I doubt it though."

"Then I cannot understand why you've added inflatable penguins to my front yard."

"They're cute!"

"That is not a good enough reason," Bryce bellowed. "Polars live in the Arctic. Penguins live in Antarctica. They have no business congregating together on my front lawn!"

"Well, I don't see why not."

"Because it makes no sense!"

"It's Christmas! Who cares?"

"Argh!" Bryce turned and stormed back toward his house.

"And you're welcome!" Jennifer hollered after him.

"I TOLD YOU THEY WEREN'T RIGHT FOR EACH other," Soraya said. "They fight like—well, not cats and dogs because cats wouldn't lower themselves to fight with the lesser beings, but like two people who really hate each other!"

Muezza let out a snort of laughter. "They've got chemistry, that's for sure."

"And it's that chemistry that will bond them for life," Bygul said. "Who wants to be with someone who agrees with them all the time? Boring."

"I think it sounds quite peaceful," Soraya said.

"You would," Muezza muttered.

BRYCE SCREECHED TO A HALT, MERE STEPS FROM his front porch.

He slowly turned and glared back at Jennifer.

"What did you say to me?" He yelled across the lawns.

"I said, you're welcome!"

"For what?" He started back toward her.

"For being awesome! For sharing my awesomeness with you! For taking your boring, stubborn ass and dragging it into the holiday spirit!"

Bryce stormed up the stairs toward Jennifer. "Say that again. To my face, this time."

Jennifer leaned up on her tiptoes, stared into his eyes and said through gritted teeth, "You're welcome."

Bryce had a plan and the plan entirely revolved around telling Jennifer exactly what he thought of her decorating madness, but when she leaned forward, he went lightheaded from the scent of her and the next thing he knew, he'd hauled her into his arms and was kissing her.

Again.

She smelled so good, tasted even better.

Dear goddess, she was *everything.*

"As I was saying," Bygul said smugly. "Chemistry."

One moment, Jennifer was all up in Bryce's space, absolutely infuriated with him.

The next, she was drowning in waves of heat, kissing him back and tearing at his clothes, desperate to be skin to skin with her mate.

Bryce grabbed her shirt and ripped it down the middle, which was like dousing the heat inside Jennifer with gasoline.

She attacked the buttons on his jeans, desperate to wrap her hand around him.

She managed to get one hand inside when he dragged her down the porch stairs and tumbled her into the snow.

She imagined she could feel it melting at her back as he followed her down, kissing her the entire way.

They rolled across the snow, clothes flying every which way, then rolled back again.

Somehow, someway, they managed to shed their clothes and then—finally—they were naked, skin to skin, writhing against each other.

"Bryce," she gasped, pulling at him, clutching at his shoulders, dragging him closer.

"One moment," he grunted, lifting just a little, then shifting so that he nestled there, *right there,* where she ached so badly.

"Bryce, now!" She pressed her hands to his backside, squeezed tight and surged upward to meet his thrust.

"Ah, goddess," he murmured as he sank deep.

"Yes!" Jennifer wrapped her legs around his waist and rolled them so that she was on top. She lifted up, then sank down, whimpering at the glorious friction that drove her ever closer to the edge.

Bryce rolled them again and settled over her, capturing her lips with his as he sank deep once more.

She cried out as he slowly worked his way over the perfect spot inside again and again and again until heat poured over her in an unending wave and the world fractured into a thousand shards of light.

Endless moments later, Bryce collapsed at her side and they lay there, the two of them breathing heavily, gasping for air, stunned silent by the power of their mating.

"What the hell just happened?" Bryce grunted.

Jennifer slowly turned her head toward him and found him staring at her, a stunned look on his face. "You had no idea, did you?"

"About what?"

"That we're mates, of course."

Bryce surged to his feet. "What are you talking about?"

"Are you serious right now?" Reaching for patience, reminding herself he was clearly a very stupid bear, Jennifer climbed to her feet and faced him. "That was no ordinary lovemaking, Bryce Meier. You may be a bear and slow on the uptake, but surely you've figured things out by now."

He just stared at her.

"We're mates, you idiot."

"How do you know?"

"I just do. Wolves usually know the minute they meet their mates."

"Bears don't," Bryce said.

"Yes, I know. According to Kate, bears are incredibly stupid when it comes to recognizing their mates."

Bryce let out a growl of annoyance. "Or maybe they're just cautious. So how do I know you're right?"

"Guess you're just going have to trust me."

"Are you serious right now? Trust the woman who tried to poison me multiple times the very first week we met? Great strategy for winning over your mate, by the way."

"Hey! I'm a very good cook, I'll have you know."

"Right." Bryce let out a snort of laughter. "And I'm the Easter Bunny."

"You're such a jerk!" Jennifer stormed toward her front door, not even bothering to grab the scraps of clothing scattered everywhere.

"Hey, now," Bryce called after her. "Don't get mad. All I'm saying is it's difficult to trust someone who's attempted to assassinate me in the past. And not that long ago, I might add, considering it was just last night you had me climbing a tree to save a cat who didn't need saving."

"Are we seriously back here again? As if you're important enough for an assassination attempt!" Jennifer flung her door open and stormed inside, slamming the door shut behind her. A few moments later, the door opened and she glared out at Bryce. "Are you coming in or what?"

Bryce grinned. "Hell yes, I'm coming in." He bounded up the stairs, crossed the porch and swept Jennifer up into his arms, kicking the door shut behind them.

Eight

THE WEEK THAT followed was one of the best of Jennifer's life.

Though Bryce continued to tease her about not being convinced they were mates, she could tell by the look in his eyes that he really had no doubts at all.

They both had to work that week—Bryce managing his family's restaurant, The Ice Box, and Jennifer working as a buyer for The Holiday Barn—which meant they didn't have as much time together as they'd had previously, but they made the most of the time they did have.

Of course, Bryce had been horrified when he discovered where she worked.

"So that's where you've been getting all those hideous decorations?" he'd demanded.

"I beg your pardon. Those decorations are the best of the season and I get a thirty percent discount and not just for me, but for family and friends too. You'd better be nice to me or I won't add you to my list."

"Harumph. That would be a blessing."

Jennifer probably should have been insulted, but for some reason, she'd begun to find amusement in Bryce's constant resistance. She was especially amused at his reaction each evening when he saw her latest acquisitions.

If he'd thought things were bad before, he'd had no idea how bad they could get.

Now that she was back at work, she was inundated with fabulous ideas for the holidays, and not just for Christmas —*all* the holidays, Shifter and human alike.

Of course, for now, she was limiting herself to just Christmas, but she had a whole line of decorations waiting in the wings for all the holidays to come.

Her biggest regret was that she would have to wait almost an entire year before she could subject Bryce to her Halloween decorations.

She could hardly wait.

If his reactions were as hilarious as last night's was to the Santa doll, she anticipated non-stop entertainment for the rest of their lives.

She'd settled the doll on the hearth in Bryce's living room and had waited with bated breath for him to notice.

It hadn't taken long and she'd dissolved into gales of laughter when she'd seen the look on his face.

"Seriously, Jennifer," he'd demanded. "Santa Claus? In white?"

"Well, they had him in the traditional red, but I thought the white was classier."

"There's no such thing as a classy Santa Claus. He's Santa and that's that. Color doesn't matter."

Whatever that meant.

She couldn't understand why he was so adamantly opposed to decorating for Christmas, especially since he'd admitted everyone else in his family decorated for the holidays.

"It's just too much work when I live alone," he'd finally said when Jennifer kept pestering him for answers.

This had made her beam with joy. "But you're not alone anymore, so hurray! You get to decorate with me!"

Bryce hadn't seemed too pleased at that response. In fact, he'd groaned rather loudly, but at that point, Jennifer decided he was just protesting for form's sake.

Which was why she continued bringing decorations home every night, up to and including the Santa doll from the night before.

Tonight's decorations were the most important though.

Tonight, they would be decorating Bryce's Christmas tree.

Finally.

It had taken all week to wear him down, but Jennifer felt he was finally ready to engage in some real Christmas spirit.

"Well, this should be interesting," Tivali said.

"Or a nightmare," Muezza muttered.

"I don't know. I guess the bear's beginning to grow on me," Soraya said.

"Really?" Bygul asked.

"Well, Shredder's starting to like him, so he can't be all that bad."

"Are you seriously judging the bear based on the psychotic cat's opinion of it?" Muezza asked.

"Yeah. So?"

"Just checking," Muezza said.

Bryce was full of nerves about Jennifer's plans for their evening.

"She's going to make us decorate the tree," he said to Shredder. "I hate decorating. I'm terrible at it and she's probably going to want the tree to be perfect and I just can't handle that pressure."

Shredder made a strange, rumbling sound in his throat and Bryce nodded as if the cat had said something brilliant. "Exactly. This is going to be a nightmare. Maybe I can just hand her the decorations and she can place them on the tree. Do you think she'd go for that, Shredder?"

The cat yawned.

"Yeah, that's pretty much what I thought. We're doomed."

At that moment, the sound of Jennifer's car turning into his driveway reached his ears. "And we're out of time to strategize, Shredder. The end is upon us."

By the time Jennifer was putting the car in park, Bryce was at her door, opening it for her. He then helped her carry in boxes and boxes of ornaments, which served to raise his anxiety to extreme levels.

He had to exert massive control over his bear because it desperately wanted him to shift and run.

Damn bear.

Lot of good it did him when dealing with a determined mate.

"Okay," Jennifer said once they had all the boxes of decorations spread out in the living room. "First rule of decorating a Christmas tree."

Bryce froze.

Here it was.

The pressure was already beginning.

"There are no rules."

Wait. What?

"The whole point is the experience, not what the tree looks like in the end. You have to get into the holiday spirit. Sing some Christmas songs and toss a few decorations on the tree. Eat some Christmas cookies and toss some decorations on the tree. Watch a Christmas movie and, you've got it, toss some decorations on the tree."

All of the angst and nerves drained out of Bryce in an instant.

Was this true?

Did the end product not matter at all?

And if that was true, why had no one ever told him?

Growing up, decorating the tree had been the most stressful experience of his childhood. He'd continually tried to balance things out, make everything symmetrical and then one of his siblings or cousins would ruin everything.

All this time and the end result hadn't even mattered?

All that stress for nothing?

Unbelievable.

Maybe he'd have to stay after Thanksgiving dinner next year to join the family in their traditional tree-decorating. He always left early, giving some excuse or another, to avoid the agony, but if it didn't matter what the tree looked like in the end, well, there shouldn't be any agony either.

Bryce felt as if the entire world had just shifted on its axis and he had his mate to thank for that.

He grinned over at Jennifer, who was flipping through songs on her phone, apparently seeking out the perfect play list.

"Got it," she said as she settled her phone on his dock and holiday music began to play through his speakers.

Seriously.

How did she *do* that?

She turned and he grabbed her into his arms and kissed her.

One thing led to another and they ended up having some truly amazing, sexy times right there in the middle of the living room floor.

Hours later, naked and quite relaxed, the two finally got around to adding a few decorations to the tree.

They watched the ultimate Christmas movie together—*Die Hard*, of course—then decorated the tree some more.

That resulted in more sexy times on the floor, then still more sexy times in the shower, then a bout in their bed before they finally made it back out to the living room to drink some wine and continue tossing decorations on the tree.

Bryce started a fire in the fireplace and they drank wine in front of the fire, watched a second Christmas movie together—*Die Hard 2,* of course—and decorated the tree a bit more.

It was three o'clock in the morning before they stumbled to bed, where they spent another hour, indulging their passions before falling asleep together.

The sound of a giant crash woke them just as the sun was beginning to rise.

They both came out of bed, disoriented and confused.

"Stay here," Bryce said as he grabbed his prize baseball bat from his closet and walked out of the bedroom.

He crept down the stairs toward where the crash had come from and toward the rustling and rattling sounds that continued even now.

When he reached the living room and saw what awaited

there, all the tension drained from his shoulders and he lowered the baseball bat.

A soft giggle came from behind him.

He glanced over his shoulder. "Didn't I tell you to stay in the bedroom?"

Jennifer rolled her eyes. "You do know I'm a wolf, right? Wolves don't hide from danger, not that Shredder really qualifies."

The Christmas tree they had spent the night decorating was now on the floor and Shredder was busy chasing several ball ornaments around the room.

"Aren't you glad the end result didn't matter?" Jennifer asked.

Boy was he ever. When he'd been in his teens, he'd sneak down in the wee hours of the morning, after everyone had gone to bed, to fix the tree.

Moving ornaments around, spreading out the tinsel, fixing all the lopsided imperfections.

He couldn't imagine how he would have felt if one of those childhood trees had landed on the floor like this.

All that perfection ruined.

"Bryce?"

"Oh, yeah. Strangely enough, I'm not even annoyed at the cat."

Jennifer giggled. "Honestly, this was our best case scenario. Because it *could* have been someone after your valuables."

Bryce leaned over and kissed her gently. "You're the only

valuable I have. Well, you and the chaos-causing cat, of course."

"What'd I tell you?" Bygul demanded. "They're the purrfect match."

"I'm starving," Jennifer announced.

Bryce grunted, then grabbed her hand and dragged her back to the bedroom. "We didn't get nearly enough sleep yet." He lifted her up and launched her toward the bed.

Jennifer let out a shriek of laughter as she landed on the bed and bounced several times.

Bryce came down over her and kissed her.

A hunger of a different sort ignited inside her as she grabbed his shoulders and kissed him back.

Bryce let out a rumbling growl, then slowly, keeping his eyes on hers the entire time, slid his way down the bed, until his shoulders were lodged between her legs.

He settled one hand on each thigh and spread them wide. He then leaned in and inhaled deeply. "Delicious," he murmured against her.

She shivered at the feel of his breath, then gasped as he took a long, slow swipe.

He let out a rumbling growl and she whimpered in response.

He nuzzled her cleft, then sent his tongue gliding through her folds once more.

"Bryce!"

He caught her clit in his teeth, tugged gently and white light sheeted across Jennifer's vision as she fisted the sheets and let out a short, sharp scream as the riptide pulled her under.

When she came back around, he was lying beside her, stroking her slowly from neck to thigh, one long stroke after another, and she found that the heat hadn't subsided at all.

It ignited in an instant, blanketing her in desire.

"Bryce," she whispered.

"Back with me?"

"Yes. Please. I need you."

He immediately rolled on top of her and lodged his cock right against her pussy. "Not half as much as I need you," he whispered in her ear as he surged forward.

The feel of him sinking deep was enough to set off another cascade of pleasure. "Bryce!"

Aa if that was what he'd been waiting for, Bryce pulled back, then surged forward again, setting a pace that erased the world until all she knew, all she felt, all she breathed in was Bryce and the absolute wonder of their mating.

Hours later, she stirred and murmured, "Still starving."

Bryce let out a bark of laughter, slapped her on the ass, then rolled out of bed. "I think I've got pancake mix in the kitchen. I'll get things started as soon as I get out of the shower."

Jennifer dozed for a moment, then realized what he'd said.

Pancakes!

This was the perfect opportunity for her to amaze him with her culinary skills. Everyone said her pancakes were the best pancakes they'd ever tasted, but a mix just wouldn't cut it.

She leapt from bed, pulled on Bryce's tee-shirt and raced down the stairs and across their lawns to her front door.

She just needed to gather the perfect ingredients.

When Bryce stepped out into the hallway, he immediately knew Jennifer hadn't waited for him.

He could smell the bacon sizzling and his stomach growled in response.

"Please, goddess of all hungry men, let her not have ruined the bacon," he muttered as he loped down the stairs and headed for the kitchen.

She'd been busy while he'd been in the bathroom.

Not only was there a huge platter of bacon—Bryce instantly swiped a piece and almost wept in gratitude as it was perfect in every way—there was also a ginormous stack of pancakes.

Bryce sniffed at them suspiciously. They seemed okay, though it looked like she'd added something to them—chocolate chips, maybe.

That was probably okay.

He wasn't a huge fan of sweets for breakfast, but he wasn't going to complain, not when the bacon was this damn good.

He grabbed another piece and set about crunching it as he helped Jennifer carry everything to the table.

Huge bowl of scrambled eggs—looked delicious and fluffy.

Giant platter of bacon—sheer perfection.

And a huge stack of pancakes.

"So," Jennifer said brightly as they sat down at the table and started serving themselves. "What do you think we should do about the Christmas tree?"

"Throw it out?" Bryce suggested.

She scowled at him. "I meant, should we just set it back up and risk Shredder knocking it down again? It's a miracle only a few ornaments broke. I guarantee that won't last, though, if the tree keeps landing on the floor."

"Maybe we should throw the tree out."

"Or maybe we should redecorate it with non-breakable ornaments. I think that would work."

"Seriously? I didn't even want to decorate the tree the

first time around and now you're going to make me decorate it again?" Bryce glared at her.

Jennifer grinned. "It'll be good for you. Practice for getting into the holiday spirit."

Well, truthfully, the experience hadn't been that bad. Especially the breaks they'd taken for sexy times.

If those were included, he could definitely get behind— "What the hell have you done to these pancakes?"

"What are you talking about? Everyone loves my pancakes!"

Bryce gagged and carried his plate to the trash, where he dumped the atrocities masquerading as pancakes.

He returned to the table with a new plate and said, "No worries. I'll just enjoy eggs and bacon this morning. Those are excellent. Maybe you should consider only cooking the things you really excel at. Leave the baked goods and pancakes to me."

Jennifer scowled at him. "I have no idea what your problem is. These pancakes are simply delicious." She took another bite as if that somehow proved something.

Bryce rolled his eyes. "I don't know why I'm surprised. We've already established you have no taste."

Jennifer gasped. "I beg your pardon!"

Nine

"OKAY, I CONCEDE," Soraya said. "Clearly those two were meant for each other."

"What convinced you?" Muezza asked.

"The bear didn't maul the wolf when she ruined his pancakes."

"*That's* what convinced you?" Tivali asked incredulously.

"Hey, bears take their food *very* seriously. Jennifer could have easily become a victim of hungry bear syndrome."

"A valid point," Bygul said. "However, we're not the only ones who have realized this. If I'm not mistaken, Shredder has finally figured out what's most important to the bear."

"Oh, no," Tivali said.

"Should we do something?" Soraya asked.

"Like what?" Muezza said.

"I don't know. Warn the wolf?"

"Now why would we do that?" Bygul asked. "This is the critical moment, when we discover whether the bear is the purrfect companion for Shredder or not."

"But what if he isn't?" Soraya asked.

"What if he is?" Bygul countered.

After breakfast, Jennifer and Bryce went their separate ways as they both had things to do before heading to work.

Since Bryce was closing that evening and would probably be getting home very late, they agreed they would just see each other the following day.

Unfortunately for Jennifer, this meant the hours stretched ahead of her once she got off work.

Deciding the key was to keep busy, she stopped at the grocery store on the way home and stocked up on popcorn, nuts and ingredients for baking.

She then spent the evening baking gingerbread cookies and chocolate toffee.

The next day, she impatiently waited for her shift to end so that she could race home, grab the bags of toffee and cookies and make her way to Bryce's house.

Surely this time he wouldn't have anything to complain about.

Even if he didn't like gingerbread, *everyone* loved toffee.

"Are you kidding me right now?" Bryce roared, glaring down at Shredder. "Why would you do this? *Why?* I was going to make my spectacular, world-famous peppermint tree candies, but now you've destroyed all my cookie cutters. How did you get into that drawer anyway?"

It was a complete and total mystery.

The only saving grace was that unlike the infamous violin, Shredder hadn't peed in the drawer. Instead, he'd puked.

A lot.

Bryce would have worried that Shredder was sick, but a quick call to his sister with a description of the puke and she'd informed him this was a normal, everyday hairball.

Apparently cats regularly puked up such offerings and Bryce was thoroughly disgusted at this discovery.

"You couldn't have puked in the litter box?"

Shredder just continued washing his nether regions without even a hint that he was listening to Bryce.

"Well, I don't know why not. If you can manage to get to the litter box in time to take care of your other business, I have no idea why you couldn't do the same when it comes time to puke up a hairball."

Silence.

"Or at the very least, puke it up on the floor, not in my cookie cutter drawer. I know it's just hair and bits of stomach acid and saliva and probably a bit of food as well, but there is no way I'm using those cookie cutters ever again. I could leave them in a vat of bleach for twenty-seven days and they would still be going in the trash. So now I have to replace all of my cookie cutters, not to mention other various baking implements." Bryce set his hands on his hips and glared down at Shredder.

"Well? What do you have to say for yourself?"

Still no answer.

Bryce let out a huff of exasperation, "Well, Jennifer's going to be here at any moment and don't think I won't blame you when she asks for cookie cutters and I have to tell her I have none."

A knock on the door came at that very moment, so Bryce leaned over and gave Shredder a quick scratch and pat on the head before heading to the front door.

The minute he opened the door, Jennifer pushed her way inside, shivering. "It's getting cold out there. Have you seen my hoodie?"

"Ah." Bryce glanced around. "Last time I saw it was in the living room when we were watching *Die Hard.*" He led the way into the living room and winced at the mess he'd been avoiding for almost two days now.

"Jeez, you never picked up in here?"

"Eh, Shredder was enjoying chasing the ornaments and batting them off the tree. I figured why bother. Found your hoodie." It looked like Shredder had dragged it into the limbs of the tree. "I think."

Bryce stepped carefully through the various ornaments until he reached the tree. He started to extract Jennifer's hoodie, but then realized it was in pieces.

"Uhh."

"What is it?"

"I think your hoodie may have become a casualty of Shredder's war against the tree."

"What are you talking about?"

Bryce started pulling pieces free of the tree. "I think this might have been a sleeve at one time." He handed it to Jennifer and turned back to the tree. "I don't even want to know how the cat managed to detach the hood, but here you go." He handed it to her as well.

Jennifer stared at the sleeve and hood in her hands, then looked back up at Bryce. "Are you sure you didn't let your polar bear out for a bit of a rampage in the living room?"

Bryce snorted. "If I'd let my polar bear out, you'd be able to tell. Trust me, there'd be way more damage than what's been done to this hoodie."

"Hmm." Jennifer stared at him suspiciously for a while, which made Bryce twitchy.

He held up his hands, palms out. "I promise, Jennifer. That right there is the work of the infamous Shredder. Just be glad you're not holding the equivalent of a violin."

Jennifer blanched. "I suppose that's true, but why was

my hoodie sacrificed? I think he should have gone after yours instead."

"Oh, believe me, he has not left my things unscathed. At all."

At that moment, Shredder came bounding into he living room, launched into the air and snagged the hood right out of Jennifer's hands.

He landed on the ground and collapsed on his side, growling and wrestling with the hood as he rolled across the floor.

"All right," Jennifer said. "I suppose it's his hoodie now."

Bryce grinned. "Very generous of you. I wasn't as gracious about my cookie cutters."

"Your cookie cutters?"

"Oh, yeah. Trust me. It wasn't pretty."

"You know, all things considered, that could have gone much worse," Tivali observed.

"So much worse," Muezza agreed.

"I'm quite impressed with the bear," Bygul said. "He didn't rampage even once."

"I don't know," Soraya said. "He lost points when he yelled at poor Shredder?"

"Poor Shredder?" Muezza and Bygul exclaimed in unison.

"He's misunderstood!" Soraya exclaimed.

"You made gingerbread cookies."

By the tone of Bryce's voice, Jennifer could tell he wasn't thrilled.

Well, that was okay.

Not everyone liked the taste of gingerbread.

"And toffee," she said. "You should try a piece."

Bryce made a face. "Not a fan."

"Of *toffee*? How can you not be a fan of toffee?"

"It's sticky. Gets caught in your teeth, makes for an unpleasant sensation."

"An unpleasant—it's a treat! It's supposed to be sweet and sticky and *delicious*."

"I'll pass."

"You suck!"

Bryce grinned. "I certainly do." He waggled his eyebrows. "Want another demonstration?"

Jennifer shivered at the memory of his mouth between her legs, teeth tugging, then lips sucking on her clit. "Ah. Maybe later. I mean. *Definitely* later. After we redecorate the tree."

"If you insist."

She shivered again. Dear goddess, just listening to his voice was enough to get her going.

"So I brought popcorn. I figured we could string it up and wrap it around the tree."

"Like you did outside for the birds and squirrels?"

"Exactly. And then I thought we could hang some of the gingerbread cookies."

"Sounds good."

"Awesome." Jennifer got holiday music going and they spent the rest of the evening laughing and playing with Shredder, decorating the tree and watching more Christmas movies, this time *Long Kiss Goodnight* and *Home Alone*, slow dancing to some iconic holiday music and indulging in more sexy times right on the living room floor.

Overall, it was a perfectly spectacular evening.

The only annoyance was when Jennifer brought out the gingerbread cookies and asked for Bryce's help in adding ribbons to the top of each so they could be hung on the Christmas tree.

She'd used her star-shaped cookie cutters and had decorated the cookies as well, which meant in her opinion, they were absolutely adorable.

Unfortunately, Bryce did not agree.

He glared at the cookies suspiciously, poked a finger at the icing and candies on top, then gave her a look that clearly accused her of attempting to poison him again.

He didn't even need to say it anymore.

She could read it on his face perfectly.

"They're delicious," she snapped at him. "I don't know why you won't at least try them."

"Maybe because everything you've offered me has been a disaster."

"Excuse me! Weren't you the one who almost broke my finger when I went for the last piece of bacon yesterday morning?"

"That was different. No baking was involved. Or ingredients now that I think about it."

"There are so ingredients in bacon!"

"Really? Like what?"

"Bacon."

"Right," Bryce drawled out the word.

"I also made scrambled eggs and you liked those as well."

"I did, but how many ingredients were in those eggs?"

"Two."

"Does that include the eggs?"

Jennifer scowled. "Yes, but what's your point?"

"My point is that you should probably limit yourself to recipes requiring one or maybe two ingredients at a time."

Arrogant, condescending *bastard*.

She was so busy fuming, she didn't notice he was getting closer until he scooped her into his arms and kissed her.

She wanted to hang onto her anger, but it was hard to think when her heart pounded and her pulse skittered and heat barreled through her like a freight train.

Damn that bear.

THE FOLLOWING WEEK WAS PRETTY AMAZING.

Jennifer and Bryce spent every non-working moment together.

They tended to move back and forth between his place and hers, depending on who was working the most hours on any given day.

Jennifer ended up buying duplicates of everything Shredder had at Bryce's house—litter boxes, cat food and dishes, cat tree, cat bed, cat toys—so that the cat could travel with them.

Of course, the first night Shredder stayed at Jennifer's house, he knocked down her Christmas tree.

Luckily she'd prepared for that and had already replaced her breakable ornaments with edible ones. She even hung a few cat toys on the tree, which Shredder took great joy in locating. Of course, he then unleashed his wrath upon the toys and they were never the same again.

Jennifer, of course, just bought him new ones.

The second night they stayed at Jennifer's house, she discovered why Bryce always insisted on wearing two sets of socks to bed.

It only took one time—one swipe of Shredder's claws aimed at her toes in the middle of the night—for her to be convinced.

It might not be the most attractive look ever—naked

with two pairs of socks—but who cared when the alternative was a cat using her toes as chew toys?

As they got closer to the Christmas holiday, work for both Jennifer and Bryce became a bit insane, which was why Bryce informed her, he hated this time of the year.

"How can you work somewhere like The Holiday Barn where you have to deal with insane people all the time and still enjoy the holidays?" he demanded.

"Because they make people happy."

"No, they make people crazy."

"Yes, crazy-happy."

Bryce shook his head and informed her that *she* was crazy.

Then he tackled her to the bed and they made love for hours.

Clearly, he wasn't too worried about her brand of crazy.

Ten

"LOOK," TIVALI SAID softly. "Shredder's definitely given them both his stamp of approval."

Jennifer was curled into Bryce on the bed, her head on his shoulder. His arm was around her waist and they were both sound asleep.

Shredder was lying on top of Jennifer's head, his nose buried in Bryce's ear, his tail wrapped around Jennifer's neck.

The entire room echoed with the sound of his purrs.

"Congratulations, team," Bygul said, "for achieving yet another pawsitively purrfect match."

UNFORTUNATELY FOR BRYCE, TIME BARRELED forward even when he was having fun and falling in love.

This meant that his doom, in the form of Christmas Eve, had finally arrived.

He had the day off work, but that gift from the goddess just wasn't worth it.

This was because it was his turn to host his family's Christmas celebration.

That horrifying, nightmarish honor came around once every six years, which was entirely too often, with nowhere near enough recovery time in between.

Because it was such a giant task hosting all the polar bears and arctic foxes in their family, the one who hosted was always given Christmas Eve off. Frankly, they needed that time to prepare, physically if not mentally—no amount of time would suffice for him to mentally prepare for the upcoming ordeal.

Still, all things considered, Bryce would have rather been at work—on Christmas Eve, no less—than have to host the yearly family celebration.

Then, as if the event weren't stressful enough, Jennifer informed him she would have plenty of time after work (The Holiday Barn closed early on Christmas Eve) to make her best Christmas recipes for the celebration.

"You know," Bryce said, trying to be as diplomatic as possible, "The Ice Box is a family restaurant, which means pretty much everyone in the family loves to cook, so they'll take care of most everything. We just have to set up the furniture, cook the meats and let them take care of the rest."

Jennifer glared at him. "First of all, by meats, I know you're including tofu, seitan and other vegetarian proteins."

Bryce grimaced. "Must I?"

"What do you think?"

He sighed. "Fine."

"Second of all, I know you hate my baked goods, for some insane reason, but everyone else loves them, so get over yourself, Bryce Meier, or you can find someone else to snuggle up to this Christmas season."

"Hey, hey, no worries, no worries. I was thinking, though, since your family's coming as well, maybe we should set up both of our yards. It'll give us more room and people can wander back and forth. I'll cook all the meats—"

She growled at him.

"And vegetarian proteins," he added hastily, "at my house and you can do all the baking over here."

"Hmm." Jennifer squinted her eyes at him, clearly trying to tell if he was being sincere or if he had some ulterior motive.

Of *course*, he had an ulterior motive, but he wasn't going to tell her that!

"Fine then," she said. "But don't get any ideas. I expect you to try my baked goods at the celebration."

Bryce couldn't possibly express the horror he felt at the idea, but he just grit his teeth, nodded and said, "Of course. I'm looking forward to it."

Christmas Day revealed a snowstorm had passed through the night before.

For one split second of joy, Bryce contemplated the possibility of his family not showing up due to the weather, but then reality set in.

His was a family of polar bears and arctic foxes. *Of course,* they'd show up, reveling and rejoicing in the weather no doubt.

His sister and her mate, along with his brother and cousins all arrived early to help him set up the tables and chairs.

"Where's Jennifer?" Zach asked, looking around.

Bryce made a face. "She's probably still baking up a storm at her place." He glanced around to make sure she wasn't anywhere nearby. "Look. Trust me on this." He leaned in close. "Those tables over there—" he pointed toward Jennifer's lawn. "—that's where Jennifer will be laying out all of her baked goods. *Don't try them.*"

"What? Why?" his cousin Wade demanded.

"Look, I'm just saying if you want to avoid food poisoning, don't sample the baked goods that come out of that house over there."

Zach made a scoffing sound and the rest of the bears rolled their eyes.

"Whatever you say, brother," Zach said. "Always did

have a weak stomach," he said out of the corner of his mouth to their cousins.

"Fine," Bryce said. "Don't listen to me. It's your own funeral."

"Probably just wants more baked goodies for himself," his cousin Luke said.

"No doubt," Zach agreed.

"Whatever." Bryce turned and saw Jennifer headed his way, so he hurried to her side and started taking her around, introducing her to his admittedly quite large family.

He'd just finished introducing her to his Aunt Edna when his cousin Steve let out a monstrous roar.

Jennifer jumped and both she and Bryce turned to stare at Steve, who stood by the tables in Jennifer's yard.

Bryce shook his head.

His cousins never had been good listeners.

"What the hell?" Steve roared. "What kind of psychotic animal puts raisins in brownies?"

Bryce let out a roar of laughter. "I warned y'all!"

"Hold up," Wade shouted. "There are raisins in the chocolate chip cookies!"

"*And* in these cinnamon rolls," Zach exclaimed.

Jennifer whirled on Bryce. "Are you kidding me? You hate *raisins*?"

"Dried up, nasty little bits of fruit? Of course I hate them! I don't know any sane shifter who doesn't."

At that moment, the wolves all arrived.

With a whoop, they descended on the table full of

Jennifer's baked goods. "Raisin cookies!" one of them crowed.

"You put extra raisins in the carrot cake, right, Jennifer?" Another one asked.

"Of course, I did."

A long, heartfelt groan came from the polar bears as the wolves all cheered.

"You know, you could have told me you hated raisins," Jennifer said.

"I thought it was pretty obvious," Bryce said.

"Not so much, no."

"You put raisins in everything, woman. You put it in the pancake batter!"

"Because they're delicious."

"You're such a weirdo." He kissed her. "But you're my weirdo, so I guess I'll forgive you."

HOURS LATER, THEY WERE ALL QUITE STUFFED AND were sitting around a fire pit—or rather, the wolves were sitting around the fire pit while the arctic foxes and polar bears were lounging in the snow.

"All right. I think it's time," Isana said. "I know you guys have been wondering who the lucky bear will be."

"What's she talking about?" Zach asked, looking confused.

Bryce just shook his head. Sometimes he really wondered how the two of them could possibly be related. "Really? You didn't see this coming?"

"See what?"

"It's been a difficult decision," Isana said. "You're all worthy, so I want to assure you, I've got a gift for each of you."

"I'm lost," Wade said.

"Me too," Luke agreed.

"Me three," Steve said.

Bryce shook his head. "I wonder if it's because you're triplets."

"What are you talking about?" Wade asked.

"Just thinking maybe you each only got a third of a brain, instead of a whole one. It would surely explain a lot."

All three of his cousins let out a rumbling growl, and Bryce grinned. "Are we gonna rumble?"

"No!" Isana snapped. "Don't even think about it. I have an announcement and you lot need to be listening."

Bryce chuckled. "All right, Isana. Lay it on them."

She glared at him. "You know I could change my mind and choose you instead."

"Good luck with that. You're not manipulating me again."

Isana's gaze shifted over his shoulder. "Or I could tag your mate."

"Don't even think about it," Bryce growled at his sister.

"What's going on?" Jennifer asked as she plopped down in Bryce's lap.

"My sister's about to hand our cousins a few gifts."

"Really?"

"Yep."

"What kind of gifts?" she asked Isana.

"The very best kind."

"Oh." By the look on Jennifer's face, she understood immediately exactly what kind of gift Isana Meier would consider to be the best kind.

From the looks on his brother and cousins' faces, they were starting to figure it out as well.

"Oh, hey, um, I think—" Wade began as he surged to his feet.

"Yeah, we've got to—" Luke spoke over him as he too struggled to stand.

"Don't even think about it," Isana said. "Sit down right now!" She waited until both Wade and Luke were seated before continuing.

"As I was saying, this was a tough choice." She looked up as Mason arrived at her side.

He gave her a nod and held his hand out.

She grabbed his hand and he pulled her to her feet, then handed her a gift bag that was clearly fairly heavy as she held it from below. "Thanks, love."

She turned back to her brothers and cousins. "Now that Bryce has adopted Shredder, I've realized we need more pets in this family. After all, who better to take care of poor homeless animals than shifters?

"So, I've decided to start this year's gift-giving with Zach."

Zach looked utterly panicked. "What are you talking about, Isana?"

"Merry Christmas, Zach." She stepped over to where he was sitting and leaning down, placed the gift bag in his lap.

He hesitated, the look on his face telling Bryce that the bag he'd thought might be moving was *definitely* moving.

With a growl of defeat, Zach removed the tissue from the bag and a tiny white kitten popped her head free.

"Congratulations, Zach," Isana said. "This cat's for you."

Read on for an excerpt from Zach's story
in This Cat's for You.

Zach was not a happy bear.

Most days he really loved his job. He was a kitchen manager at The Ice Box and worked the dinner shift, which allowed him to sleep late.

Unfortunately, today wasn't one of those days.

His older brother Bryce was out for the next two days which meant Zach had to take over some of Bryce's management duties at The Ice Box, including getting up at an ungodly hour to go in and get the restaurant ready to open.

He hated mornings. He hated opening. And he hated the lunch shift.

In other words, today he hated his job.

This was why he parked in the alley and entered The Ice Box from the back.

It was also why he didn't turn on any lights as he headed down the back hallway toward Bryce's office.

It was because he was in a bad mood that he didn't notice the lights at the front of the restaurant were already on or that the light inside Bryce's office was also on.

It was because he was in such a shitty mood that he din't register the sound of a voice crooning softly from inside Bryce's office until he was halfway through the room.

And it wasn't until he was almost to Bryce's desk that he realized he wasn't alone in that room.

It was only when he saw the epic ass lifted into the air, pointing out from under his brother's desk that he realized he wasn't alone and it was only then that he registered what he was hearing.

"Aren't you the sweetest things I have ever seen? And you are the best mama ever."

Staring at that quivering ass encased in the tightest skirt he had ever seen, Zach felt a wave of heat like he'd never experienced wash over him. Who was this woman and why was she in his brother's office?

"Such a good mama, taking such precious care of your babies. Yes, you are."

There was something familiar about her voice, but he could't quite figure out what it was. Her head was under the desk so he couldn't really see much.

"They're so lucky to have you. Yes, they are. Such sweet babies. Such a good mama."

All Zach could really see was that amazing ass and those incredible, shapely legs and those heels.

No.

The only one he knew around here who wore heels like those was—

It couldn't be.

She wiggled her ass again and another wave of intense heat rolled through him and his polar bear suddenly woke, swiping out with his claws.

Damn. He had to get her out from under that desk before he lost control of his bear.

Zach cleared his throat loudly.

The woman froze for a moment, then slowly wiggled her way out from under the desk.

Zach stared as if in a trance, unable to look away as she slowly, slowly backed out, sank back on her heels and looked up.

Lumiki.

His baby sister, Isana's best friend.

A girl he'd grown up with.

Someone he'd always treated as another little sister, someone he was afraid he'd never see in that same light again.

She was also the hostess for The Ice Box.

"Hi Zach."

"Lumiki." His voice was rough. He cleared his throat, then held out a hand and helped her to her feet. "Ah. What were you doing?"

"Oh! You have a mama cat and kittens." She beamed up at him.

He shook his head. Surely he hadn't heard her right. "What?"

She waved a hand at the desk. "Look! Aren't they adorable?"

He turned and stared.

"Ah, fuck."

Lumiki gasped. "Zach!"

"What? You cannot believe this is a good thing."

"Of course it is! They're adorable and need someone to take care of them."

"Yes. And I know exactly who to call for that."

Lumiki looked devastated at that statement, but he couldn't let that sway him.

Zach had to somehow do all the management crap Bryce usually took care of *plus* his own job today.

He didn't have time to take care of a bunch of kittens.

Besides, this was a restaurant, not a rescue center.

Unlike his sister's place, since she actually ran one of those.

Five minutes later, he couldn't believe his ears. "But I'm your brother! Where's the family loyalty, Isana?" He paced back and forth in front of his brother's desk, trying to ignore Lumiki, who was back under it, cuddling kittens and crooning to their mama, and more importantly, trying to ignore her epic ass.

A practically impossible feat.

"It's because you're my brother that I can, Zachariah. I know good and well that you will take care of that mama and those kittens and ensure they're safe and snug and well-fed through the holidays. Do you know how full my shelter is right now? I'm bursting at the seams! There's just no room, Zach. The mama obviously feels safe in the office right now and that's good enough for me. Just make sure she has enough food and water and the temperature is kept cozy for her. Bring in some blankets so she can snuggle and make a nest for herself and her babies. Get a litter box and just let them be."

Zach groaned. "A litter box?"

"Yes. One with low enough sides the kittens can climb in it. When they're old enough for adoption, I'll help you find homes for them. I promise."

Zach's eyes narrowed. He heard something in her voice that didn't exactly inspire confidence. "Homes that aren't mine, I presume."

Isana let out a tinkling giggle. "Now, Zach, you know I've always said bears would make the worst pet parents."

"You *used* to always say that," he growled darkly. "Then you mated a grizzly who happens to enjoy playing papa bear to a bunch of cats."

"Yes, well, Mason's quite the unique bear. Now, call me if you have questions about how to care for the kittens and good luck. Love you."

"Wait, Isana—"

But it was too late. She'd already hung up.

Zach let out a low growl then dropped his phone on the desk, which prompted a loud hissing sound from beneath it.

"Sorry, sorry." He leaned over the desk to look down at

Lumiki. "Well, you got your wish. Isana can't take them, so we're stuck with them."

"Yay!" Lumiki backed out from under the desk and beamed up at him. "They can be our restaurant kitties!"

"What? Are you crazy? Not a chance. We're finding them homes as soon as they're big enough to be separated from their mom."

Lumiki climbed to her feet and glared at him. "That's not very nice."

"You should be happy I'm letting them stay at all. If Bryce were here, they'd probably already be outside in the alley."

Lumiki raised an eyebrow at him.

"Well, unless someone told Isana." He groaned. "And someone *always* tells Isana."

Lumiki giggled.

Zach narrowed his eyes at her. "And don't think I don't know who's to blame for that! Crazy foxes. Just for that, you're elected for kitten care."

"No way! I will *share* the care with you, but I'm not taking it on all by myself. And just to be clear, I live in an apartment and I see where this is going. There are five kittens plus mama cat under there, so don't even think of trying to get me to adopt all six at the end of this. It's not happening."

Zach barked out a laugh. "Okay. All right. Fine. How about this? We work together and get my cousins to adopt them all."

Lumiki narrowed her eyes at him. "Which cousins? You have like a bazillion."

He grinned. Couldn't argue with the truth. "The bear ones."

She snickered. "You really think you can convince Wade, Steve and Luke to adopt them all?"

"Nope. Doesn't mean it won't be fun trying."

She giggled. "Okay. Let's do it."

"Excellent." Zach thought about it a moment, then grinned. "I think we should make a game of it."

"What?"

"No. A wager."

"A wager?"

"Yep. Whoever gets the most kittens adopted wins."

Lumiki eyed him suspiciously. "Wins what?"

A ton of truly lascivious, wicked things raced through Zach's mind all at once, but that wasn't why he'd suggested this wager.

Was it?

Oh goddess, maybe it was.

"Zach? What exactly are we wagering?"

"What would you like to wager?" He asked huskily.

She licked her lips, which just gave him all kinds of dirty ideas. "I'm not sure."

"Winner's choice?" He suggested.

She hesitated.

"We've known each other a long time, Lumiki. I would never hurt you. You know that, right?"

"Of course, I know that, Zach."

"So?"

She nodded. "Okay. Winner's choice."

"Shake on it?" He held out his hand.

She slowly slid her hand into his.

They had touched each other a million times over the years.

A casual arm around the shoulders.

A hug.

A kiss on the cheek.

A nudge of the shoulders.

A hip check.

A friendly slap to the back or punch to the arm.

This handshake felt like none of those.

There was something there that he'd never felt before.

Something new.

Something electric.

And he could see by the look in Lumiki's eyes, she felt it too.

It was the start of something new.

Something that might just change their lives forever.

Grab your copy of This Cat's for You today.

Please consider leaving a review on your favorite book site.

If you would like to be notified of

Pepper's new releases, please sign up here:

www.peppermcgraw.com/newsletter

Join Pepper's readers group on Facebook:

www.facebook.com/groups/theshenanigancrew

Other Books by Pepper

THE MURRYSVILLE COALITION

The Crazy Cheetah Lady

One Sad Kitty

A PAWSITIVELY PURRFECT MATCH

Catnapped

The Real McCat

Unbearably Cute

A Catmas to Remember

This Cat's for You

Santa Kitty

Hocus Purrcus

Tridents & Tails

Abra-Cat-Abra

Satan's Kitty

Valen-Cats

Vampurr Lovin'

A Beautiful Cat-ship

Grave Cattitude

THE SHENANIGANS SERIES

Shifter Shenanigans

Witchy Shenanigans

Full Moon Shenanigans

Hotel Shenanigans

Dragon Shenanigans

Undercover Shenanigans

Spooky Shenanigans

Holiday Shenanigans

Valentine Shenanigans

Lucky Shenanigans

STORIES OF THE VEIL

Guardians of the Veil

Astra

Glory

Luna

Zara

WICKED

No Rest for the Wicked

Wicked Is As Wicked Does

Anthologies & Collections

PAWSITIVELY PURRFECT TRILOGIES

THE CAT'S MEOW

Catnapped | The Real McCat | Unbearably Cute

HOLLY JOLLY PAWLIDAY

A Catmas to Remember | This Cat's for You | Santa Kitty

SHENANIGANS ANTHOLOGIES

CRAZED

Books 1-3

AMAZED

Books 4-6

HOLIDAZED

Books 7-10

SHENANIGANS

The Complete Collection

STORIES OF THE VEIL

THE UNVEILED

Astra | Glory

THE VEILED

Luna | Zara

WICKED DUET

WICKED

No Rest for the Wicked | Wicked Is As Wicked Does

About the Author

WWW.PEPPERMCGRAW.COM

PEPPER MCGRAW is a USA Today Bestselling Author of paranormal romance. Her life to date has sadly been paranormal-free, but she knows it's simply a matter of time before her fated mate finally appears. Until that glorious day arrives, she keeps herself busy writing (and reading) paranormal romances.

Pepper loves animals, especially cats, and spends her free time volunteering at local shelters and for Trap-Neuter-Release programs. She's had the supreme honor of winning occasional head butts and meows from the local ferals in her neighborhood and has even convinced a few to come inside and adopt her as their own.

bookbub.com/authors/pepper-mcgraw

facebook.com/ShenanigansSeries

goodreads.com/peppermcgraw

instagram.com/peppermcgraw_author

tiktok.com/@peppermcgraw

twitter.com/peppermcgraw